DARE

IN SAFE HANDS
BOOK 2

S.M. SHADE

This is a work of fiction. Names, characters, businesses, places, events
and incidents are either the products of the author's imagination or used
in a fictitious manner. Any resemblance to actual persons, living or dead,
or actual events is purely coincidental.

Cover art by Ally Hastings at Starcrossed Covers.

PROLOGUE

DARE

I can't believe what I'm hearing. My little sister, Leah, sits across from me, tears trickling down her cheeks. She's eighteen years old now, but I'll always see her as the little girl who followed me around. Since the day she was born—two days after my fifth birthday—I've looked out for her, protected her. I tried to keep anything bad from happening to her.

I failed.

"When, Leah? When did he hurt you?"

Her hands fidget in her lap and she stares at the floor. "Every time I went to visit. You know, when he and aunt Gena would babysit for me."

"Why didn't you tell me, or Mom, or someone?"

"He said if I told, everyone would be mad at me, that I'd break up the family. I thought Dad would never forgive me. I tried to tell Mom, but...she didn't believe me."

It suddenly makes sense why she's telling me now. Dad died two years ago, and we moved away. We haven't seen his brother, my uncle Howard, since the funeral. "Mom invited them to come and visit. They're supposed to stay a week! I can't avoid him for that long. Please, can I stay with you until they leave?"

My little sister has just told me our uncle sexually abused her for years, and my mother knew. All I can see is red. How the hell did I miss this? I spend my days and half the nights tracking sexual predators, but I didn't see what was happening right in front of my face. "Is he at Mom's house now?"

"Yes." She sniffs and sits back on the couch. "He smiled at me. This creepy fucking smile like we have some special secret. Please, Dare, I can't stand to be around him."

"Of course you can stay here." She'll probably be staying permanently now. No way do I want her going back home with Mom. I wrap her in a hug. "I don't want you going back there. Stay here. I'll go get you some clothes and anything else you need for the week."

"Thank you." Dark circles ring her eyes.

"Go lie down in the guest room and take a nap. You look exhausted."

Nodding, she heads for the bedroom, and I grab my keys. I should call Landon, or any of the guys and get a plan together for how to deal with this. I know I should, but all I can see is my golden haired baby sister being abused by that monster. I've never had a problem with my temper before, but the rage now pulsing through me is uncontrollable. I don't want to control it. I'm going to kill the son of a bitch.

The drive to my mom's house is a blur. I don't know if I stopped at the lights and stop signs or blew right through them. All my focus is on finding him and making him pay. As soon as I hop out of the car, I see him sitting on the front porch swing, Leah's favorite place to read. He smiles at me, and my blood heats to boiling.

"Derek! I haven't seen you in forever. You sure bulked up."

One look at his pocked face and oily gray hair is all it takes for me to lose the last of my control. My fist connects with his face over and over again, until I can barely discern his features from the blood. I feel his jaw crack beneath my fist, but it isn't enough. Not nearly enough.

Dragging him into the yard, I can vaguely hear Mom yelling, but it doesn't register. I don't talk to him. There's no cursing or demanding answers. Anything he says will be a lie. I let my foot do the talking, kicking him in the ribs, and when he curls up, trying to protect himself, I land a few good ones on his back.

It takes two cops to pull me off of him, but by then, he's an unrecognizable bloody pile in the yard. From the back of the cop car, I watch the paramedics strap him to a gurney and put him in the back of an ambulance. They don't cover his face, so I assume he's still alive.

I'm taken to the police station and booked, locked in a cell with a few other guys who look like they've had an equally shitty day. I'm a big guy. Add to that the fact that I'm covered in blood, and I can understand the wary glances from the other prisoners. They're afraid.

That cell is home for two days until a judge sets my bail and explains the charges against me. Attempted murder. I guess the asshole survived.

My best friend, Landon, shows up that evening to post my bail. He's waiting by his car when I emerge from the jail, a grim look on his face. "Are you okay?" he asks.

"I'll be better after a cheeseburger and a shower," I reply, climbing into the passenger seat.

"You want to tell me what the hell happened?"

"He was abusing Leah. She told me it's been going on since she was eight."

Landon curses under his breath. "I contacted Mason. He has the best lawyers, but…attempted murder, I don't see you escaping this without doing some time, Dare."

"I know. I just need to get a few things arranged before I do."

Leah can't go back home to a mother who let this happen. Thanks to my hacking skills, I have plenty of money, some from legitimate work, but more stolen from credit card thieves online. I have no problem stealing from thieves, especially thieves with bank accounts totaling in the millions. I'll pay up my rent ahead of time, and Leah can live in my house while I'm locked up.

The state wastes no time taking me to trial, and though the jury doesn't come back with a guilty verdict on attempted murder, they find me guilty of aggravated assault. The judge sentences me to five years, which means I could be out in three with good behavior. It's worth it.

Leah is safe living in my house and going to a nearby community college. Landon will keep an eye on her while I'm locked up. Her abuser is permanently confined to a wheelchair, paralyzed from the waist down.

I knew that last kick to the spine was a winner.

CHAPTER
ONE

AYDA

You know it's going to be a good day when you start it by falling out of bed. In my defense, some jerk startled me from a vicious dream by pounding on the door like the cops. Before I was really awake, I tried to leap from the bed, which isn't recommended when the sheet is wrapped around your feet.

So, here I am, a grown twenty-four year old woman lying on the floor amid a puff of dust bunnies. I really should clean under my bed. The pounding resumes, and I make my way through my apartment to answer the door, where a disgruntled delivery driver thrusts a clipboard at me. "Sign here."

My eyes struggle to focus since I didn't grab my glasses, but I manage something akin to my signature. A box is shoved into my hands and the nominee for friendliest delivery man is off without so much as a *"have a nice day."*

"Fuck you very much," I grumble, tossing the box into my office. All this for printer ink. A glance in the bathroom mirror makes me laugh. No wonder the guy couldn't wait to escape. In addition to the usual ugly I carry, my face bears a large pink imprint of my wrinkled pillowcase. Wild, dark curls spray in every direction and my stretched out T-shirt makes me look like an over-grown child.

Well, that's what he gets for waking me at the crack of noon. I retrieve my glasses and grab a yogurt for break-fast, flopping in front of the TV while I eat. A few minutes of the so-called news is all I can take. Besides, it's sunny out and there won't be many more days like this. Indianapolis seems to go from ninety degrees to snow overnight.

My apartment overlooks the pool, and since it's the middle of a weekday, there are only two people swim-ming. It's a good time to work on my tan. I throw on my bikini, grab a large towel, my phone, and a bottle of water, then head downstairs.

The pool is a typical apartment complex pool. Rectangular, with a set of stone steps disappearing into the shallow end. It's surrounded by deck chairs with a few umbrellas thrown in for those who don't worship the sun like I do. In a few hours, the pool will be brim-ming with swimmers and sunbathers, and you couldn't pay me to come then. The stares and murmurs ruin the experience. People are ridiculous.

It's all clear now except for a young mother—I think her name is Sunny—and her toddler. We've spoken a few words in the past and unlike most people, she doesn't question me. I give her a smile while she coaxes her son to jump into the water, and she waves.

I settle on a lounger, put in my earbuds, and push play on the new Hozier album. I'm totally in love with this man's voice. Nothing beats lying there, eyes closed, and losing myself in the music. This is one of my favorite ways to spend my time, especially on days like today.

The sun warms my body, and a light breeze dries the sweat on my skin. I could stay here forever. Summer is over, but Mother Nature doesn't seem to notice, and the temperature climbs into the mid-eighties. A dip in the pool is definitely called for. The water is warm, almost too warm, but I know the breeze will cool me once I'm wet. After swimming a few laps, I sit on the steps, letting my legs dangle in the water.

Sunny's little boy dog paddles over to me. "I swim!" he exclaims with a grin before climbing the stone steps to stand beside me. His grin widens, and he puts two fingers in his mouth. I know the second his gaze lands on my scars. "You have boo boo?"

Sunny catches up with him and instantly apologizes. "Ayda, I'm sorry. Brody, don't bother the nice lady."

"She has boo boo," he announces, his face pinched with concern. "Owie? I kiss?"

"It's okay. They're old boo boos," I reassure him. He's so sweet. "They don't hurt. No owies."

He squirms and protests when he's scooped up into his horrified mother's arms. "Brody, hush."

"It's fine," I assure her. "It's sweet of him to want to help. He's really learning to swim, isn't he?"

Her smile displays the pride she feels. "Like a little

fish. I'd better get him in for a nap or he'll be a beast. It was nice to see you."

"You too."

"No nap!" Brody cries, and Sunny rolls her eyes, carrying him out of the pool.

I have the place to myself, so I spend another thirty minutes basking in the sun before heading back to my apartment. A cool shower feels even better than the pool, and I revel in the sensation of the chilly water washing over my scalp, taking the heat of the day down the drain. My growling stomach reminds me all I've had to eat is a container of yogurt. A package of sliced turkey makes my mouth water when I look in the fridge. Sandwiches, it is then.

I quickly throw together two turkey, lettuce, and tomato sandwiches, placing one in a baggie. After finally locating a storage container to match the lid—how the hell do I end up with too many lids?—I spoon in a double helping of potato salad and seal it up. The sandwich, potato salad, and a bottle of water go into a plastic bag, along with a spoon. My plate gets a temporary spot in the fridge while I run the bag downstairs to the parking lot.

"Tucker? Are you here?" The stench from the dumpsters is sickening in the afternoon heat. I'm glad to see Tucker isn't hidden behind them. His sleeping bag and blankets are folded up between the dumpster and the wooden enclosure surrounding them, so he isn't far away.

I met Tucker a few months ago when I was taking out the trash. We started chatting, and while he won't let me take him to the mission or a homeless shelter, he will accept food. Once a week or so, he uses my shower while I wash his clothes and blankets. I keep hoping he'll let me get an agency involved and get him off the street, but he doesn't want that.

"Hey there, Ms. Ayda," Tucker calls. He's found shelter from the sun under a tree.

"Hey, I brought you some lunch. Are you staying cool? It's brutal today."

"It's got nothing on Afghanistan. I'm fine." He accepts the bag of food. "Thank you."

"You're welcome. Take care of yourself." I always feel guilty leaving him out here, but he's a grown man. There's little I can do.

I'm waiting on my photo editing software to load when Sadie calls. Filled with indecision, I hesitate over the accept button before I finally tap it. "About time. What are you doing?" she asks.

"Just finished lunch and thinking about getting some work done. What are you up to?"

"Leaving my last whiner of the day. Lunch at four-thirty? Are you ever going to keep a healthy schedule?"

Sadie is a physical therapist and all around health nut. I met her five years ago and hated her with a passion. To be fair, she was twisting and pulling my body to keep the skin pliable around my scars. It's hard to like someone who's torturing you. We eventually grew close throughout my rehab and became friends.

"I keep a schedule. Bed by three a.m., up by noon, eat when hungry. Seems to keep me alive."

"Whatever. Let's go out for a drink tonight."

This is the reason I hesitated to answer my phone. Sadie is always trying to pry me out of the house to do things I'm not comfortable with. I know she means well, but parading around in public while people talk shit isn't my idea of a good time.

"Not tonight. I have two ads to design and a ton of emails to answer."

"Said the liar," she scoffs. "Fine, meet me at the studio tomorrow night after closing?"

"I'll be there. I've been working on some new choreography."

"All right, woman. I'll let you work, but if you don't show tomorrow, I'm hunting you down." A squeal of brakes is followed by a string of swear words.

"Sadie? Are you okay?"

"Some shit for brains just cut me off! Hey! Yeah, suck a bag of dicks, buddy!"

"Sadie!" I can't help but laugh.

"I've got to go. See you tomorrow, chick."

The girl is crazy, but I love her. What I'd do to be that fearless.

After the slight interruption, it's time to get back to work. Over the past few years, I've managed to build a successful online business which offers graphic design and marketing help to small businesses.

The artistic aspects are more enjoyable than the marketing, but I've learned that an eye-catching ad is a powerful tool. Creating images that draw the eye and captivate an audience comes naturally to me. Best of all, I never have to leave the house.

It's after midnight when I close my laptop and crawl into bed. Hmm…e-reader or TV tonight? I've been binge watching a show with a cute British detective, so TV wins.

No sooner than the episode starts playing, the moaning begins. Great. New neighbors moved in last year, and for a luxury apartment, our walls are really thin. Based on the things I've heard, my bedroom, bathroom, and kitchen share a razor thin wall with Mr. Fucks Everything next door.

We've never met, but I've caught glimpses of him coming and going. It's clear why he has no shortage of women. At least six foot four with broad shoulders and a full sleeve of tattoos, he's got that dangerous look too many women fall for. Me included.

Turning up my TV is futile. Instead, I kill time by playing around on the internet for a few minutes. Hopefully, they'll make it a quickie. The fake, high pitched cries grow until I have tears in my eyes from laughing. Amateur porn has better acting. A woman's voice cries, "Yes! Oh, yes!" Then a shrill screech pierces my eardrums.

"For fuck's sake!" I exclaim, maybe a bit louder than I intended. Especially because the room falls dead silent right afterward.

A rumbling laugh cuts through the plaster, and a deep voice responds, "Sorry, sweetheart. Didn't mean to disturb you. You can go back to your show."

His smug voice pisses me off. He must be able to hear my daily life as well as I do his. Boring as it may be. I'm not deigning to answer him, choosing instead to crank up my music to a level that drowns out any further noises.

After half an hour, I turn off the music and go back to

my show. "Are you finished getting revenge on me?" the asshole asks.

I'm sitting in bed, leaning against the wall, and judging by how clearly he can be heard, he's right on the other side of it. "Nothing I do is any of your business and certainly doesn't have anything to do with you."

"Maybe you don't like hearing me fuck because you aren't getting any."

My cheeks heat with anger. "Maybe you're a cocky asshole who thinks far too highly of himself."

"I'm definitely cocky. What's your name?"

I massage my temples with my fingertips. "Will you just shut up and pretend we can't hear each other?"

"If you tell me your name."

"It's Ayda." My frustration is obvious with the sigh that accompanies my response, but it doesn't deter him.

After a few seconds of silence, he asks, "Don't you want to know mine?"

"Not really."

"It's Dare."

"Of course it is. Gang name or general alias?"

His laugh rumbles through the wall. "Short for Derek."

"Great. Nice to meet you. I'm going back to my show now that the porn sounds have stopped."

"Jealousy is such an ugly emotion."

Ugh! This man is so infuriating! "Go fuck yourself."

"That's your department, sweetheart. Your vibrator isn't as quiet as you think it is."

Damn it. I never even thought about that. What kind of jerk points that out?

"No reply to that one?" he presses.

Nope. Not answering. Pissed off and embarrassed, I press play and try to focus on my show. My mind keeps wandering, and I catch myself trying to picture him in his room. Is he asleep? Stretched out in bed wearing boxers? Naked? My dirty mind just has to go there. He wasn't far off earlier when he said I need to get laid.

Twenty minutes later, I give up and turn off the TV. I'm starting to doze when he speaks up again. "Good night, Ayda."

Asshole.

The sound of thunder shaking the apartment wakes me. Torrential rain rattles the windows while I flop onto the couch with a piece of toast and a new book. Stormy days are meant to be spent curled up on the couch with a good book. The wind has knocked my internet out, so I feel totally justified in taking the day off from work.

After a few hours, I manage to drag my lazy ass from the couch to the bathtub, soaking until the water gets cold. A dull roar from next door tells me Dare is taking a shower. My mind instantly conjures up images of him, all naked and wet, probably getting ready for a date. I haven't been on a date in five years, and I don't see it happening anytime in the near future. He hit a nerve when he said I'm jealous. Not of him, but of anyone who has a normal sex life when chances are I never will.

It's times like these I try to count my blessings. I'm alive, and generally in good health. The scar tissue causes me some pain, but nothing like the agony I survived after the burns. I have enough money to take care of myself, a roof over my head, food in my stomach, and a good friend. That's more than a lot of people ever get, and I'm grateful.

Without brooding any further about my permanently single status, I pull on my jeans and a t-shirt. It's after nine when I grab my duffel that holds my dance gear and head out the door. The good thing about being a night owl is that there's never much traffic to deal with. Only ten minutes after I leave the house, I'm unlocking the door to the On Pointe Dance School.

The last class ended at eight, and the place is dark and silent. I flip on the lights, illuminating the shimmering wooden floor and wall to wall mirrors. Sadie's sister, Lisa, owns the studio, and when Sadie found out I used to dance, she arranged for me to come after hours to practice as part of my rehab. That was a few years ago. Lisa has since given me a key and permission to come at night. She also asked me to consider a job teaching here, but I'm not ready for that.

I'm happy practicing alone, or occasionally with Sadie. I began attending ballet lessons when I was eight and fell in love with it. When I'm dancing, I don't feel the pull of skin or the pain that comes along with it. There's only the floor beneath my feet, the wind whipping across my body, the music filling the world with beauty.

When I emerge from the dressing room in my leotard and tights, Sadie is digging through a box of CD's. "Hey girl, want anything in particular?"

"Anything is fine until we're warmed up. I brought my iPod for the choreography I want your help with."

"You know I can't choreograph to save my wide ass. You should come during business hours and have Lisa help."

"I'll think about it," I lie. We laugh and chat while we run through our stretches and warm up at the barre.

While I adore dancing, it's bittersweet. I'd been accepted in the corps de ballet for a prestigious dance company in New York when Talbot took that chance away from me forever. It's taken years to get to the point where my body can handle ballet again, but I'll never get full range of motion back. Add that to the fact that ballet is about beauty—the beauty of the dance and the dancer—and you can understand why my plans changed.

Still, dance is my escape, and when Sadie and I leave a few hours later, I'm exhausted, sweaty, and perfectly content.

I'm starving when I return home. Dancing always makes me hungry. It's also the reason I can pretty much eat whatever I want without gaining weight. It makes up for the fact that my job is so sedentary.

A thump rattles the kitchen, followed by the sound of a chair being scraped across the floor. What the hell is Dare doing over there? I probably don't want to know. A mixture of male and female laughter leaks through the wall from next door while I fry some sausage and peppers. Great. He'd better not keep me up all night with his bedroom antics.

Two scrambled eggs get tossed into a skillet before I add the sausage and peppers to make an omelet. I can't stand to eat eggs for breakfast, but dinner is another story.

"Damn! Something smells good," Dare announces. "What are you cooking?"

He's so loud he could be right beside me instead of standing in his kitchen on the other side of the wall. Ignoring him, I slide the omelet onto a plate, grab a glass of grape juice, and head to the living room. My favorite show is on, full of zombies and gore.

By the time it's over, my eyes grow heavy, and I move to my bedroom. One of the comedy podcasts I listen to has released a new episode. Awesome. Snuggling under the covers, I'm ready to listen.

I've never been able to fall asleep quickly. My brain won't cooperate, choosing instead to dredge up the past. It's easier to fall asleep with something playing to distract me, a TV show, podcast, or audiobook. It doesn't matter which as long as I can listen to something other than my own internal dialogue that's so depressing. It's weird, because while I'm not exuberantly happy, most of the time I'm content.

"What the hell are you listening to?" Dare's voice rumbles through the wall.

Really? Can't he just pretend that he can't hear me? We've done it for nearly a year. The best plan is to ignore him.

"Ayda, I know you're there."

I could switch to headphones, but they aren't comfortable to fall asleep in, and why should I change anything for an obnoxious neighbor anyway? It's not like it's blaring. It's doubtful he can even make out the words at this volume. He's being an ass.

"What is your fascination with British shows? Everything you listen to has an accent."

I'm not engaging him.

"Is it a porno? Do I get to hear your vibrator tonight?"

Ugh! "I don't watch porn!" I snap, forgetting I'm supposed to be ignoring him.

A deep chuckle follows. "Nothing wrong with porn."

"Can't you just shut up?"

"What were you cooking? It smelled great."

"You seriously want to have a conversation through this wall?" I huff, pausing the podcast.

"Or I could come over." The delicious threat delivered in that deep come-fuck-me voice makes me shiver. It does more than that, if I'm being honest with myself. I haven't had sex in five years, but not because I want to be celibate. My sex drive is fine, but it's hard enough for a beautiful woman to find a man who won't jerk her around, much less a scarred mess like me. Hence the vibrator.

"No!"

"Okay, then. What did you have for dinner?"

"A sausage and pepper omelet."

"Sounds good." I hear a faint scrape and picture him leaning against the wall, maybe sitting on his bed. "Do you want to know what I had?"

"I'm going to assume the reason for this questioning is so you can tell me that you ate pussy."

His laughter rings out loud. It makes me wish I could see his face when he laughs. It's such a great sound. Smooth and deep. I wonder if he has a dimple when he smiles? Ugh, he's getting in my head.

"That wasn't what I was going to say. I had leftover pizza, actually. I'm not much of a cook."

"Hmm, too bad." Yawning, I turn to lie on my side.

"A nice neighbor would invite a poor bachelor over for a home cooked meal." The amusement in his voice makes me smile, despite my aggravation.

"Well, I bring food to the homeless man who sleeps

by the dumpsters. Maybe if you wait out there, I'll bring you a sandwich sometime."

"Harsh, Ayda. Now I'm really hurt."

My eyes won't stay open anymore. "Good night, Dare."

"Good night, Ayda."

CHAPTER
TWO

DARE

"Derek!" My sister, Leah, barrels into me as soon as I enter her house, wrapping her arms around me. She's the only one who still calls me Derek. Her gaze is filled with barely restrained excitement.

"Hey, kid. Are you ready to do this?" I know she's grown now, nearly twenty-two years old, but I still don't like the idea of her moving so far away. She's spent the past few years taking classes at a nearby community college, and now she's moving a state away to work toward a doctorate in psychology.

"All packed up!"

A small, rented moving truck sits by the curb, packed and ready to go. I'm driving the truck so she can drive her car. After locking the door and leaving the keys in the mailbox for the landlord, she darts to her car. "Keep to the speed limits!" I call, climbing into the truck to follow her.

Rolling her eyes, she dismisses my warning with a wave of her hand. I pull out behind her and a few minutes later we're cruising down the highway. Summer stubbornly hangs on with its heat and humidity, though Labor Day is right around the corner, and I wipe at the back of my neck with my palm. For the money I paid to rent this damn truck, you'd think the air conditioning would work. All it blows is hot, stinking puffs of air.

Highway driving is dull and monotonous even with my favorite playlist blaring, and my mind begins to wander. Right to Ayda. Messing with her through the wall has been the most fun I've had in a long time. I've always been able to hear her, but it never occurred to me to talk to her. Maybe because I was too busy listening to her with her vibrator and trying to picture the look on her face when she comes.

She's so introverted, staying in her apartment most of the time. I assume it's because she's self-conscious. I've seen her a few times, lying beside the pool, or coming from her car, but I don't think she noticed me. Her eyes were always trained on the ground like she hoped to find a wad of money on the pavement, her long hair hanging half in her face. It wasn't until a few days ago when she was talking to the homeless man in the parking lot that I saw her smile and got a glimpse of why she hides herself away.

Crinkled skin, somehow warped and bubbled, extends from the corner of her jaw up to her temple on the right side of her face. It must be from a burn. I don't know how long she's had it or what happened, but she's obviously not comfortable letting people see. I can't blame her. People can be assholes.

I was staring at her, but not because of the scar. It was the expression on her face while she spoke to the homeless man. A man the rest of us have completely overlooked. It wasn't a look of pity or disgust, but compassion and understanding. She cares. And that's a hard damned thing to find these days.

Leah puts on her turn signal, and I follow her small silver car onto the highway ramp and through a neighborhood dotted with apartment buildings. Instead of living in the dorms, she's opted to share an apartment close to campus with two of her high school friends. Neither are present when we arrive, but the apartment is already lightly furnished with their belongings.

"Are you sure you don't want me to stay until one of your roommates shows up?" I ask when she starts unpacking her boxes.

Getting to her feet, she approaches me and lays her hands on my shoulders, looking up at me. "I'll be fine. You have to quit worrying. I've been on my own a few years now, you know."

"I'm aware." My gaze sweeps around her bedroom before I continue the search out in the hall. "Do you have a smoke detector?"

Laughing, she rolls her eyes. "Yes, right there." She points to a detector in the center of the hall ceiling. "And there's a carbon monoxide detector in the kitchen and a fire extinguisher under the sink. Now, get going or you'll have to drive the whole way back in the dark."

"Fine, I know when I'm not wanted." She squeals when I dig my fingers into her ribs, tickling her like I did when she was a kid. When I stop, her demeanor turns serious.

"Thanks Derek. For everything. I know how much you sacrificed to save me, and I promise I'll make you proud. I'm going to work with kids who were hurt like I was."

My throat tightens, and I pull her into a hug. "Just live your life and be happy, kid. That's all I want."

She squeezes me, then steps back. "I am happy."

"And stay away from boys."

"No problem. I prefer men now."

"Real funny, critter."

"Don't call me that!" She shoves me, laughing, then returns to unpacking.

"See you, Leah."

"Bye," she calls, her head buried in a box.

The drive back is interminable, but after seeing where she lives, I'm not as worried about her. She's happy. Maybe I should try for a little happiness myself.

The past year since I was released from prison, I've been partying. It was an attempt to make up for all the lost time, to block out the memories and the misery of those gray walls. I've never had trouble attracting women, and since I put on about twenty-five pounds of muscle while I was locked up, it's become even easier. My bedroom has been a revolving door of women, mostly one night stands I picked up at a bar. Just a little fun for both of us with no strings attached. I thought I was happy, that getting laid and hanging out with my friends was enough, but now I'm not sure. It feels like something is missing.

My work makes me happy. In Safe Hands—or ISH—

is the best thing I've ever done, made even better because I started the organization with my best friend, Landon. Jeremy and Justus came along later. They're just as dedicated and trustworthy, which is a necessity when hunting down online predators and child molesters. All of us have hacking skills which help keep us anonymous and allow us to aid the police while also hiding our own criminal activities.

We *are* criminals—never doubt that—but I've never hurt anyone who didn't deserve it. We're largely funded by our ability to hack the hackers and steal their funds which are mostly gained from the sale of credit card and bank account numbers. I never have to worry about money. Our main concern is not getting caught when we dispose of the predators who don't go in our reports to the cops.

Repeat offenders and child molesters of the worst kind aren't reported. Most have done multiple stints for horrible acts against children and the system has failed to lock them up for good. Sometimes, the justice system fails, and we step in to clean up their mess.

It's late when I get home and without the guys here, it seems so quiet. We've recently moved ISH from my apartment to a house Landon inherited from his uncle, and while I'm glad to have my place back to myself, I'm not used to silence. Prison was always loud, with prisoners yelling and banging around all day and night. All I wanted when I was inside was a few minutes of quiet, but now I'm not sure how to deal with it.

I grab a cold piece of leftover pizza from the fridge and take a bite while kicking my shoes off, then plop onto my bed. As soon as my back hits the wall, I can hear

Ayda's TV. The opening theme song for The Walking Dead plays, reminding me I'm about to miss my favorite show. Grabbing my remote, I flip to the correct channel. While the commercials are playing, I can't resist talking to Ayda, curious whether she'll still respond.

"I'll bet Daryl is your favorite, isn't he? Probably the reason you watch the show."

The sound of an exasperated sigh reaches my ears, and I think maybe she's going to ignore me this time when she finally replies, "Actually, I like Michonne."

"So you're into women."

"If I say yes, will you leave me alone?"

"Hell no. I'd love to see you with a woman."

"Trust me, you wouldn't," she snorts. "And just to make sure that image is wiped from your brain, I'm not into women."

"Probably better in the long run. I don't like to share."

"Are you going to shut up when the show comes back on?"

"Come over and watch it with me." The words jump out of my mouth before I can think about the consequences. I learned a long time ago not to sleep with women I work with or live near. It causes too much drama when it's over. And there's no way I could have this woman beside me on my bed without fucking her.

"Not going to happen."

"Then we'll have to watch it together like this."

"Whatever blows your skirt up," she says, amusement in her voice.

I'm winning her over, getting her to talk to me, but why? Why am I determined to pursue her when she has no interest? I may have just answered my own question.

I want her because she doesn't want me. She isn't going to trip over herself to get to me or go out of her way to do what I want like all the other women I've been with. Plus, she has an amazing little body.

We fall silent when the show comes back on, engaged by a world of the undead. When they break for ads again, I remark, "He's a dead man. They're finally going to kill him off."

"Bullshit. He's a first season character. This isn't Game of Thrones."

Holy shit. She watches my other show too? I'm not a big fan of TV but those are the two shows I try not to miss. "If you tell me you're a Lannister fan..."

"Nope, Targaryen all the way."

"I can live with that." Her giggle puts a smile on my face. "You should read the books," I advise.

"You read?"

"Try not to sound so shocked." I read everything I could get my hands on while I was locked up, but I'm not volunteering that information.

"I'll do my best...shh, it's coming back on."

Silence descends again until I exclaim, "What the fuck?" at the same time she shouts, "Holy shitballs!"

"Shitballs?" I repeat, seized by laughter at her choice of curse word.

"The kid got his head chomped on!" she defends.

"You're right. Shitballs is fitting."

When the show ends, the sound of her TV does as well, and I hear her bed creak. "Going to sleep now?"

"If my infuriating neighbor will allow me."

"Your infuriating neighbor can come over and make sure you sleep well. I've got the cure for insomnia."

"In the same place you keep a plethora of STD's, I imagine. Good night, Dare."

"Good night, Ayda."

———

The scent of cinnamon wafts through my kitchen the next morning, making my mouth water. Ayda must be baking, and it smells amazing. Leaning against my counter, I pour a cup of coffee and tap on the wall. "I smell French toast."

"No," she replies. "You smell cinnamon rolls."

"Don't you know how cruel it is to tempt a man with baked goods and not share?"

She doesn't reply, and I hear her shower kick on, effectively ending my teasing. Oh well, I have shit to do today that doesn't include the obstinate girl next door. After a quick shower, I text Justus and arrange to meet him at the gym.

Unlike Landon, Jeremy, and me, Justus has a moral objection to taking stolen money from the credit card scammers unless it's used to help a victim. He chooses instead to work as a stripper. He must be good at it, because I've seen the ridiculous amount of money he pulls in. We all like to give him shit about it. I mean, one of our best friends shakes his cock in people's faces for money. That shit is just funny.

The toe of my shoe comes into contact with a sealed plastic container when I step out of my door. I've noticed containers like this left at Ayda's doorstep before, and now I know it's because she gives food to the homeless man who lives in the parking lot. Maybe he returned the container to the wrong door? That idea is quickly squashed when I pick it up and realize there are two large cinnamon rolls inside. Ayda left me breakfast. Why didn't she knock and hand them to me?

I learned long ago not to try to analyze the perplexing minefield that is the female thought process, so I scoop up the rolls and take them with me, eating them both before I make it out of the parking lot. Damn, they're good.

Justus hops out of his truck when I arrive, his mop of blond curls whipping in the wind. "Hey, lovely locks."

"Fuck off, Hulk." He pulls his hair back and wraps a black band around it.

"You're just jealous because my dick is bigger around than your bicep."

"And yet, I still get mine wet way more often."

Laughing, we head inside. I began working out in prison because it was about the only thing that passed the time other than reading. It surprised me how quickly I grew to love it, and one of the first things I did when I got out was sign up for this twenty-four hour gym. Justus and I go a couple of afternoons per week, and I also meet Landon here for a few nighttime workouts since he can't go out during the day.

Landon has a rare disease that forces him to stay out of the sunlight. He deals with it well, but it also isolates him, so I try to get out with him at night when I can. Since he's met his girlfriend, Zoe, he's been pretty occupied which means I'm back to working out during the day.

We hit the weights first, spotting each other, then head for the treadmills for some cardio. "What's up your ass today?" Justus asks. "You're in your own little world. Do you need to get laid that bad?"

"Fuck you. I'm thinking. I realize that's a foreign concept to you." Actually, my mind keeps wandering to Ayda. I haven't once spoken to her face-to-face, but she won't get out of my head. It's strange that she'll talk to me but doesn't want to meet. Maybe an outside opinion on it would help. "You know the girl who lives next door to me?"

"The one you can hear using her vibrator?"

Damn, why did I ever tell him that? "Yeah, we've been hanging out...sort of."

"What do you mean sort of?" He increases the speed and incline of his treadmill, and I do the same, matching him.

"We can hear each other through the walls, especially in the bedroom. We talk and watch TV and shit."

Justus raises his eyebrows. "You only talk through the wall?"

"So far."

"Do you even know what she looks like?"

"Sweet, tight little body, an ass you want to take a bite out of."

"What are you waiting for?"

I wipe my forehead with the back of my hand. "She's my neighbor. If she turns out to be a psycho, I'll never get away from her."

"That's true. Why only talk through the wall? Ask her to come over, see if she's crazy before you fuck her."

"I plan to. So far, she isn't having it."

Justus throws back his head, laughing as he steps off

of the treadmill. "Dare finally has to chase a woman. Priceless."

"Why do I tell you anything?" I growl, accompanying him to the locker room.

"No idea, dude."

My stomach is growling like a pissed off bear when I leave, so I stop at a burger joint on the way home. After ordering a double bacon cheeseburger with fries and a drink, Ayda's voice pops into my head, telling me she feeds the homeless man who lives behind the dumpster. Turning back to the drive-thru speaker, I add, "Actually, double that order."

The homeless man sits on the curb in the parking lot, a tattered paperback book in his hand when I pull in, the greasy bag of food on the seat beside me. I'm not sure how to go about this without making him feel like I pity him. I know if someone pitied me it'd piss me off.

"How's it going?" I ask, feeling mildly like an idiot. It's obviously not going well if he's here instead of eating dinner in an actual home.

"Can't complain," he replies, a guarded look on his face as I approach.

I take a seat on the curb beside him. "Burger place screwed up and doubled my order. Want a burger? It's just going to get thrown away."

His expression tells me I'm not fooling him, but he nods. "I could eat." He looks surprised when I divide up the food, then proceed to eat instead of going inside. "Thanks."

"No problem."

We eat in silence, catching a few stares from other

tenants returning home from work. "People can't mind their own damn business, can they?" I grumble.

The man laughs. "That's all you. People look right through me."

I've been guilty of that myself. I have no idea how long he's been living out here. If I'm being honest, I probably never would have talked to him if it weren't for Ayda bringing him to my attention. His clothes are dirty and wrinkled, and it's clear from the jut of his collarbones he doesn't get enough to eat, but his posture and the way he holds himself screams soldier.

"Iraq?" I murmur.

"Afghanistan."

"How long have you been back?"

"Six months." He gets to his feet and chucks our food wrappers into the dumpster. "Thanks for the burger. I have to go."

My hand darts out like it has a mind of its own. "My name's Dare."

He shakes my hand. "Tucker."

"Good to meet you. I'm in apartment 2B if you ever want to have a beer."

"Sounds good, thanks."

———

It's past midnight when Justus rings my phone. "What do want, stripper?" I ask, annoyed he's interrupted my nightly conversation with Ayda.

"Have you heard from Jed lately? I've been trying to reach him all day."

Jed lives in a farmhouse ISH bought years ago. He

takes care of the place and raises the pigs who help us dispose of the remains of die-hard pedophiles. He's around sixty years old, but still sharp as ever. We met him a few years ago, tracked him down, actually. It was all over the news that someone was killing sex offenders. Just making their way down the registry.

His granddaughter had been kidnapped, raped and killed when she was ten, and though her murderer is doing life in prison, Jed realized there were many who weren't. And the government kept a nice little hit list for him. When he found out who we are and what we do, he was happy to help.

"I haven't heard from him. Do you want to head out to the farm? Make sure everything is alright?"

"I think we'd better. I'd take Landon, but he's holed up with Zoe somewhere."

Scrubbing my face with my hands, I accept the fact it's going to be a long night. "Come and get me. I've had a few beers."

"On my way."

I lean my head back after disconnecting the call. "I have to go. Raincheck on the next episode?" I ask Ayda, through the wall.

"Sure. Is everything okay?" She barely knows me, but I can hear the concern in her voice. She's compassionate.

"Probably. A friend of mine hasn't been answering his phone. He's getting older and lives alone. My friend Justus is coming over to get me so we can check on him."

"Oh, I hope he's all right."

"Thanks. Good night, Ayda."

"Good night, Dare."

Justus shows up a few minutes later, and I hop into the passenger seat of his truck. "Were you sleeping?"

"Nah, talking to Ayda."

Justus shakes his head with a grin. "Through the wall again? You realize that's fucking weird, right?"

"I've tried to get her to come over, or to invite me over. She's kind of introverted."

Justus laughs. "Isn't prison supposed to harden you, not soften you up? The old Dare would've charged into her apartment and made himself at home."

"I don't want to scare her, but believe me, I'm close to doing just that." Pulling out my phone, I try to call Jed again. "Still no answer. He could be passed out drunk."

"Most likely."

But we both know we can't take that chance. It's unlikely that anyone has connected Jed to ISH, but not impossible. If some hacker or predator has gotten to him, they'll wish they hadn't. I trust Jed. He'd never lead them to us or tell them anything.

The drive takes over an hour, and it's something is wrong as soon as we pull up to the house. Jed's dog, a lab mix with the eloquent name of Humper, runs to meet us, whining. Jed never leaves Humper outside overnight.

Justus rubs behind Humper's ears. "Hey there boy, where is he, huh?"

Humper follows us to the door, and wiggles impatiently while Justus unlocks it. The house is dark and chilly, an open window letting in the cold air.

"Jed? It's Dare!" I yell. "Where are you?"

Justus gives me an anxious glance when there's no reply. A flip of the living room light illuminates a perfectly normal scene. Jed's cigarettes and lighter are on the table by his well-worn leather recliner, the TV remote resting beside them. "I'll check upstairs," Justus says, and I nod, heading for the kitchen.

As I open the pantry door, Justus yells my name. Taking the stairs two at a time, I find him with his hand on his forehead, standing at the edge of Jed's bed. Despair shines from his eyes when he turns to me. "He's dead."

"What the fuck happened?"

"There's no blood or anything. I think he died in his sleep. I'm going to call an ambulance. Will you look around outside, make sure nothing is out of the ordinary? They'll probably send cops since it was an unattended death."

"Yeah, sure…are you okay?"

Justus was closer to Jed than the rest of us, and often spent the night here, drinking and playing cards with him. "I'm fine."

He's lying, but he obviously wants to be alone a moment, so I call Humper to join me and make my way outside. The barn is open, and the pigs haven't been fed. I quickly slop them before locking up. The shed is secure, and there are no missing tools or equipment as far as I can tell. The wail of a siren reaches my ears. The ambulance arrives a few seconds later, its lights throwing red streaks across the darkened farmhouse.

"Upstairs," I inform the two young paramedics. "When my friend didn't answer his phone, we came to check on him and found him like this."

It doesn't take long for the medics to pronounce him dead and arrangements are made for the coroner to retrieve the body. Two officers arrive and take a look around before taking our statements. "No, he has no family to notify," Justus explains to the officers. "We'll take care of him."

"Sorry for your loss," one the officers mumbles, before they leave.

The coroner removes the body and informs us where to go to make arrangements. There's a good chance they'll want to do an autopsy first since he had no medical conditions as far as we know.

Justus sits on the steps, staring into the distance at the rising sun. "I didn't know he had no family," I remark, sitting beside him.

"He had a daughter, but she killed herself when her little girl was murdered. That's why he was so devoted to ISH. His life wasn't easy."

I lay a hand on his shoulder. "He was a hell of a guy, and he spent his last years doing exactly what he wanted to do. Helping rid the world of child predators. He went in his sleep, the way we should all hope to go."

Justus nods, his hair falling over his forehead. "Yeah. A hell of a guy." He turns to me. "After we get him taken care of, we have to find someone to watch the farm."

"We'll take care of it. One thing at a time. Let's go tell Jeremy and Landon what's happened and see what we need to do next."

CHAPTER
THREE

AYDA

I hate to admit it, but I've started looking forward to my nightly conversations with Dare. It's nice to have a man to talk to, someone who likes the same shows I do. Over the past month, he's invited me over to watch TV and tried to get me to invite him countless times, but I don't want to ruin this. The way things are now is good. We can talk about our favorite shows and books, and I can laugh at his jokes without worrying about keeping my face turned away or wondering how disgusted he is by my marred skin. It works. We've never met, and as soon as he sees the woman that he's been spending so much time with, it'll come to an end.

My protesting muscles make me groan when I climb out of bed. I've been dancing much more than usual, spending time at the studio about four nights a week working on choreographing a new number. Sometimes it feels like a waste. No one will ever see it or know the hard work I put into it, but it doesn't matter. I dance for me, for my own health and peace of mind.

I've barely dried my hair after my shower when Sadie knocks on the door. When I open it, she flounces in with a wide smile. "Good. You're ready. I figured you'd try to back out again."

"Nope, a movie sounds great." I think I've pushed Sadie to the end of her rope lately, canceling plans or finding a reason to turn her down. I don't want to lose her friendship. Tonight, I'm determined to go along no matter how uncomfortable I feel in public. Besides, theaters are dark. There shouldn't be too many whispers or stares to deal with.

I grab my coat then follow her out to her car. A chilly breeze blows my hair into my eyes, and I tuck it behind my ear. The weatherman has predicted below average temperatures this week and apparently he's right. A shadow flashes beside me. It's Tucker, making his way back to his sleeping bag. He must be cold and probably hasn't eaten all day.

"Tucker!" I call, heading over to him.

"Hey there, Miss Ayda. You look pretty. Going out tonight?"

"I'm going to a movie with my friend." I hold out my spare apartment key. "My apartment will be empty for a few hours. Why don't you get a hot shower and wash your stuff? There's a big pot of chili in the fridge. Just needs popped in the microwave."

Tucker hesitates, surprised I'm offering him a key. "That's really kind of you, but I can't—"

"Also, my toilet has been running something awful.

I'd hate to have my water bill skyrocket. Maybe you could have a look at it?"

His hand goes to the back of his neck, giving it a rub. "I—yeah, I can take a look at it." He takes the key with a smirk, letting me know I haven't fooled him one bit. "Thank you."

Sadie stares at me with her jaw agape when I return to the car. "Did you give him a key?"

"Yeah."

"To your apartment?"

"Yes." I should've known she'd freak out.

"You gave a homeless man a key to your apartment?"

"Nothing gets past you."

She holds up her hands. "Oh no, you don't get to bring the sarcastic Ayda out to play on this one. This is serious. What if he robs you? Or lays in wait for you to come home and decides you're going to give him more than food?"

Laughing, I fasten my seatbelt. "He won't even take money from me. He's not going to run off with my computer."

"Maybe he'll just settle for a piece of ass," she argues.

"I can't give that away," I snort. "He sure as hell isn't going to take it."

Her face darkens as we pull out into traffic. "There are plenty of guys who would love to get with you. You don't give them a chance."

"Whatever. The point is, he's a decent guy who's having a hard time. I'd want someone to help if it were me."

Sadie smiles softly. "Sometimes, you're too damn nice for your own good."

"Noted. What movie are we going to see?"

"Your choice. I can't decide between the new Kevin Hart comedy and a romance with Channing Tatum."

"Comedy. I'm not a big romance fan."

I used to adore a good love story, but I don't watch them anymore. It's too depressing and only reminds me what I can't have. There were two main things I wanted in life when I was young: a career in dancing, and a loving family. Any hope of either was stolen from me by one competitive bitch and her devoted, psycho boyfriend.

The movie is funny, and we have a good time. Some of the lewd jokes made me snort with laughter and my first thought each time was that Dare would like it and probably have a crude add-on to contribute.

Sadie drags me to a little restaurant that's famous for its chocolate cheesecake, and we both order a slice. "Look out hips, here it comes," I remark with a grin, taking a large bite.

"Spare me, you skinny bitch," she scoffs. "I swear, I was walking through my house the other day and saw something out of the corner of my eye. I had to take a few steps back and stare at the wall to realize it was the shadow of my ass, following me."

"Men love that ass, though."

"Yeah, they do," she replies, grinning around a bite of cheesecake.

"I've been talking to someone...sort of," I blurt. I don't know why, but I'm desperate to tell someone about Dare.

Her mouth forms an O, and she places her fork on her plate. "Details. I want details right now. This is fantastic! I was starting to think you'd never get back in the game."

Slumping back in my seat, I shake my head at her enthusiasm. I couldn't ask for a better friend. "Don't get all excited. It's not like…we're not dating or anything."

"But you're hanging out?"

"Sort of."

She frowns. "Sort of? How do you sort of hang out with someone? Are you stalking him?"

"No!" I throw my napkin at her. "He lives next door and—"

Her hand clamps onto my arm. "Tell me you're talking about that mass of tattooed bad boy I saw leaving the apartment next to yours."

"Uh, yeah. His name is Dare."

Customers turn to look at us when she lets out a squeal and stomps her feet under the table. "He's gorgeous! Shit, I'd dare. You hang out and talk?"

"Our walls are thin, and we can pretty much hear everything the other person does, so we started talking."

"Wait." She holds up a palm. "You only talk through the walls?"

"I know it's not exactly normal."

"Has he tried to meet you in person?"

Uh-oh. I shouldn't have said anything. "He's mentioned it a few times."

"Then why haven't you?"

I give her a *don't be stupid* look and get a glare back in return. Before she can speak, I shake my head. "Just don't. I like talking to him. He's fun and interesting. We both keep late hours. I'm happy with how things are now and if he meets me, I'll lose it. It's pathetic, I know."

She sighs. "It's not pathetic. If this guy has won you over just by talking through a wall, he must be something special, and I think you should give him a chance. Face to face."

"And if he runs once he sees me?" I snap.

"Then he's a dickhole and I'll tell him that to his face, right before I kick his balls into his throat."

See why I love her?

Her hand closes over mine. "I honestly don't think that'll happen, though, Ayda. I've told you before, no one is as conscious of your scars as you are. If he's a good guy, he won't care. He'll see how beautiful you are. And if he doesn't, you're better off without him, as a friend or anything else. I know you. I know you want more, but you'll never have it if you don't take a chance and put yourself out there."

I know she's right. I've been alone too long and grown so accustomed to it, I didn't even realize I was lonely. His smooth voice has filled an empty place I didn't know I had, and a small, aching part of me wants to believe I could have more than his words.

"I'll think about it," I reply in a near whisper.

"Good, now let's get out of here."

Her words run through my head all through the ride home and while I let myself into my apartment. It's only a matter of time before he sees me anyway. I mean, he lives next door. It's amazing we haven't met face to face yet. Still, my urge to delay the inevitable as long as possible still exists.

My apartment is empty. A note from Tucker waits on my kitchen counter, telling me my toilet is fixed and thanking me for the food. The laundry room smells faintly of detergent. He must've washed his clothes and bedding. I'm usually most comfortable when I'm alone, but tonight, my place seems hollow and empty.

Dare's apartment is quiet when I climb into bed. A few minutes of straining to hear if he's home are fruitless. Disappointed at the silence I'm greeted with, I turn on my tablet and load one of my podcasts. There are a few new ones waiting for me since I haven't listened in a while. With Dare to chat with until I fall asleep, I haven't needed the voices to chase away the dark thoughts and loneliness.

It's nearly three in the morning when my brain gives up the fight against sleep.

———

It's a rainy day, perfect for catching up on work. I designed a book cover for an independent author last month and apparently, she's been raving about my work, because eight more requests wait in my inbox. After finishing a few ads for a local candle store, I work on book covers until it's late enough to go to the dance studio.

Lights chase each other across the ceiling of the expansive studio when I flip a switch, illuminating the empty space, made larger by a mirrored wall. A smile rises on my lips. It makes me long for the classes I took when I was young, before we became so competitive, when it was just a bunch of girls having fun doing what we loved. Those days hold some of my best memories.

The routine I'm working on now has turned out better than I hoped, and I can't wait to show it to Sadie.

Just as I finish and collapse to the floor to catch my breath, a voice makes me jump.

"That was amazing."

Sadie's sister, Lisa, approaches me. "Sorry, I didn't mean to scare you. I came back because I forgot my phone." She waves a purple phone. "How long have you been working on that?"

"A month or so." I shrug, not thrilled about being watched when I didn't know it.

"We have a competition coming up and that routine would be perfect for one of my students. Would you mind?"

"Of course not," I reply, thrilled someone will get to see my work even if I'm not the one performing it. "I've recorded it a few times to watch for my mistakes. You're welcome to it."

Lisa follows me back to the dressing rooms. "I know you said you're not interested in teaching, but hear me out. I have a twelve-year-old male student named Ryan, who's struggling. He recently came out to his classmates and it didn't go well. They were already giving him shit for dancing, as you can imagine."

"Kids that age aren't known for their compassion," I agree.

"Take Me to Church would be the perfect song for him to perform to. I'm sure he can relate, and the passion he'll bring will knock the judges out of their seats. I love what you've done with it, and it'll fit perfectly in the contemporary dance category."

I know what's coming next.

"But it would be much better if you could teach it to

him, correct him where he needs it, instead of learning from a video."

Damn. "I really don't think…"

"He could come in on the slow hours, between our scheduled classes if that makes you more comfortable. I swear, he's the sweetest kid."

Double Damn. How can I say no? "I'll come in and meet him if you want, see if he wants me to teach him."

"Are you kidding? He's going to love this routine! Thank you. I'll call his dad tonight and see when he can bring him in."

"His dad brings him to class?" I ask, surprised.

"Yeah, single dad. His mom ran off a few years ago."

"Poor kid."

"He's got a fire in him, though. You'll see."

She accompanies me out to the parking lot once I get dressed, and I give her my cell number. "I'll let you know when he can be here," she assures me, rushing off with a smile on her face.

Regret sets in before I even make it home. It's not that I don't want to work with the kid, but I dread returning to the dance world—even in such a limited way—after being out of it for so long. Chances are, I won't see anyone I used to know. It's been six years since I was attacked, and though it made headlines, I doubt most people would remember, even with the effects clear on my face.

It's after midnight when I get home, and a light rain begins to fall. The street light is out, and I almost miss the massive figure slumped on the steps leading to Dare's place.

Shit. It's him. What the hell is he doing sitting in the

cold rain? He doesn't move. Part of me wants to keep going and hope he doesn't notice me, until I hear him snore. He's passed out. I can't just leave him there.

"Dare?" His eyes fly open, and his hand wraps around my wrist when I shake him. It takes him a second to focus, then a goofy smile stretches across his face. He loosens his grip on my wrist, and I pull it back. "What are doing out here?"

"Beautiful night," he slurs, closing one eye when he looks up at me. Even rimmed with red, his eyes are gorgeous. Pale blue that appears silver in the glare of the streetlight.

"It's freezing, you idiot. You need to go inside."

Stumbling to his feet, he grins down at me. "Let's go."

"Inside your own apartment. Alone," I explain, trying not to laugh.

His expression darkens and a fleeting sadness flashes in his eyes. Since he makes no effort to move, I grab his hand and pull. It's laughable. The man is a damn mountain. There's no way I can budge him. He seems to find it funny too, chuckling as he throws an arm around me.

"Come on. Get upstairs before you fall down them," I sigh, leading the way. I need to get him into his apartment before he passes out again. With any luck, he's drunk enough that he won't remember this.

Swaying on his feet, he leans his head against the apartment door and mumbles, "Keys are in my pocket." His eyes are closed. Rather than argue with him, I slide my hand into his front pocket, but only find a wad of cash. I'm rewarded with a mischievous grin when I try his other pocket and pull out his keys.

"I knew you wanted to get in my pants." Hot breath that smells of whiskey flows across my neck, and I feel his body pressed against my back when I unlock his door.

God, he's a solid wall of muscle. I can't let him see he's getting to me. "Shut up and get inside."

His living room looks like a typical bachelor pad with a long sectional couch, coffee table, and a huge TV. I only get a glance before he wraps an arm around my shoulders, then heads down the hall. He bumps his bedroom door open with his foot and flops onto the bed, taking me with him.

Oh no. No, no, no.

"Where you think you're going?" he slurs, after I roll off the bed and get to my feet. "Stay with me."

"You're drunk."

"You're sexy."

A giggle escapes me. "You have no idea what you're saying, and I'm sure you'll regret it tomorrow...if you even remember." Please, don't let him remember.

"I finally got you in my bedroom. I'll remember."

With no concern whatsoever, he shucks off his jeans and pulls his shirt over his head, tossing it to the floor. His eyes fall shut, and I take the opportunity to escape the bedroom in search of ibuprofen. He's going to have one hell of a hangover when he wakes. His bathroom is bright and clean, painted the same pale yellow as mine. I'm standing in the bathroom of the most gorgeous man I've ever held a conversation with. I can't help but have a look around.

Fine. I'm snooping. Don't judge me.

His medicine cabinet holds the usual male items,

aftershave, a razor, an extra toothbrush. A bottle of ibuprofen hides behind a stick of deodorant, and I spill a few pills into my hand before going to the kitchen. There are bottles of water in his fridge, but not much else. He wasn't kidding when he said he doesn't cook.

He's in the same place I left him when I return, eyes closed, his body laid out like a starfish. Fuck, I've never seen so much muscle in one place. My eyes are drawn to his thighs first, lying like tree trunks on the dark sheets, then travel up over his boxer briefs, taking in the clear outline of a cock that definitely matches the rest of his thick body.

A chuckle rattles his chest, and he peeks at me with heavy eyelids. "Are you going to stand there eye-fucking me all night, or get into bed?"

Busted.

"Neither," I reply, trying to act like he didn't catch me drooling over him. "I brought you some water and painkillers."

When I bend to put them on his nightstand, he grabs my arm. His gaze meets mine for a long moment, and he slowly reaches to cup my face. His palm slides over the scars on my cheek, caressing them, and I close my eyes. No one has touched my face since the attack. I'm not sure how to react. Hoping I won't be met with a disgusted expression, I force my eyes to open and see nothing but sympathy in his.

"How did this happen?"

My walls slam back into place when I realize what I'm doing. What he's doing. "Go to sleep." My voice is barely more than a whisper.

"Good night, Ayda," he murmurs, as I make my way toward the door.

"Good night, Dare."

My mind is races after I crawl into my bed. He didn't cringe when he saw my face. Was it just because he's drunk? I didn't imagine the way he was looking at me. He was serious about wanting me in his bed, but there was no way I was going to take advantage. What if he didn't remember when he woke up? Trying to find a nice way to kick an ugly girl out of your bed makes for a particularly awkward morning after. Besides, even if I wasn't scarred, this guy is way out of my league.

The best thing I can do is pretend nothing happened and hope his brain was whiskey soaked enough to block out tonight.

———

"Uhh."

My eyes open to the sound of a loud groan, and I can't help but laugh. Dare is paying for that binge now.

"Are you laughing at me?" His voice is low and full of gravel. Sexy. My mind instantly jumps to the sight of him in his boxer briefs last night. Hopefully, he's forgotten everything.

"Not everything is about you, you know."

"Thanks for getting me inside last night."

Damn it.

"You really didn't have to strip me. I feel so violated."

"Shut up. You know I didn't touch you."

"It's just a matter of time, babe."

If he only knew how badly I want to touch him.

"Don't you have a job to get to or something?" Actually, I have no idea what he does for a living. His hours are as erratic as mine.

"Or something," he agrees. "I'm bringing you dinner tonight."

"No thanks."

"Do you like Italian?"

I'm seriously going to strangle him. Instead of arguing, I ignore his last question and go take a shower.

Today is Halloween, and I need to buy candy for the trick-or-treaters. After getting cleaned up, I make a quick trip to a nearby store. After tossing a few big bags of candy into my cart, a display of chocolate cupcakes shaped like bats catches my eye. I've already made a watchlist of horror movies on one of the streaming services I subscribe to, so my evening plans are decided. Cupcakes, chocolate, and gore.

The day passes quickly, and it's barely dark outside when I get the first knock on the door. Sunny greets me with a smile, and her little boy, Brody, holds up a plastic pumpkin.

"Hi, Ayda. How have you been?" Sunny asks. I haven't seen her or her son since the day we ran into each other at the pool.

"I'm good. How about you?"

"Good. He keeps me busy." She grins down at Brody, who's wearing an Elmo costume. "What do you say, Brody?"

"Candy!" he demands, holding up his pumpkin.

"Trick or treat," she corrects him.

"Close enough," I laugh, giving him a handful of candy.

"We started a little early. He couldn't wait."

After hesitating for a second, I ask, "Would you like to come in and have a cupcake?"

"Sure." Smiling, she grabs Brody's hand and leads him inside. While he sits on the living room floor devouring a cupcake, we chat and get to know each other. "He's going to get that everywhere," she worries, glancing at her son, whose chin and nose is now coated in chocolate.

"Don't worry about it. I need to mop anyway."

"So, what do you do?" she asks.

"I'm a graphic designer."

"Really? That's awesome. I don't have an artistic bone in my body."

"What do you do?"

"I work at The Children's Museum."

My jaw drops while I turn toward her on the couch. "I used to love going there when I was a kid!"

"It's a pretty great place to work. They have a built-in daycare. It saves me a ton on babysitters." She seems to sense the question I'm hesitant to ask. "His dad isn't in the picture anymore. He didn't want the responsibility."

"Oh, what an asshole."

We both burst into laughter. "Yeah, that's a pretty good description," she agrees.

A knock at the door gets me to my feet, and I grab the bowl of candy, prepared for more trick or treaters. Instead, I'm nearly bowled over by two tons of sexy man in a black suit.

"Dare! What are you doing here?"

"Bringing dinner. You don't listen too well, do you?" His smirk turns into a smile when he sees Sunny gazing at him with her jaw hanging. I'll bet that's exactly how I looked the first time I saw him. He puts the bags he's carrying on the kitchen table, then turns to stick out his hand to Sunny. "Hi, I'm Dare."

Her cheeks redden as she shakes his hand. A pang of pure irrational jealousy floods through me. Sunny is beautiful, with blonde hair and pretty blue eyes. She's tall and curvy, everything I'd expect a man like Dare to look for in a woman, and I suddenly feel like a grungy loser.

"Sunny," she replies, before turning to regard me. "I live in the next building, apartment 3B. Come by some-time. I'm always stocked with junk food." Her sincere smile draws the same from me. She's really nice and funny. And I definitely need to make some friends.

"I will." I grab a paper towel for her to wipe Brody's face. "Bye Brody. Hope you get a bunch of candy."

They make their way down the stairs, leaving me alone and face to face with Dare.

"You didn't have to bring dinner. I mean, just because I unlocked your door for you last night doesn't mean you need to do anything. It was no big deal." Great. I'm babbling. I can hear the tremble of nerves in my voice. No doubt he can too.

I don't want to lose what I have with him, as pitiful as that may be. The best thing to do is treat him like I would any friend and let him see I don't expect anything more from him. That's not exactly easy to do when he's standing before me in a black suit I want to tear off of him.

His expression is serious when his gaze locks with mine. "I don't do anything I don't want to do, Ayda."

Christ, I know what I want to do, but I doubt it's what he has in mind. Not anymore. "Okay."

"Now." He unpacks the bag and places two large containers on the counter. "I've got spaghetti and chicken alfredo. Plus, some garlic bread."

"It smells fantastic." I retrieve two plates and some silverware. "There are water bottles in the fridge, or soda if you'd rather have that."

"Water's fine." It's funny how fast we fall into sync, and my nerves calm down. We've spent hours talking through the walls, and this feels no different. We take our food to the living room to eat in front of the TV.

"Pick a movie from my watchlist if you want," I tell him, motioning to my TV before running to answer the door again to dole out more candy.

When I return, he's chosen the vampire movie that was listed first. "Why are women so into necrophilia?"

"What?" I ask, sure I heard him wrong.

"Why do women want to fuck dead dudes?"

"Hey, these vamps don't twinkle or fall in love. And I don't want to fuck them."

"Good to know." He takes our dishes to the kitchen while I deal with another group of trick-or-treaters.

This time I open the door to a group of teenagers. The two girls are dressed as what I assume are strippers, although one wears a headband with cat ears attached. The boys haven't bothered with a costume, though they've splashed some fake blood on themselves and one has a bunch of latex hanging off of his face.

"Trick or treat," one of the girls says, and I dutifully add candy to their bulging grocery bags.

"Thank you," the same girl says, before they turn to leave.

As I'm shutting the door, I hear one of the boys laugh. "Damn, did you see her face? It was scarier than your mask."

They all laugh, and another boy replies, "Yeah, but there's no peeling that shit off."

People talk shit, and teenagers more than most, so I try to shake it off. I'm used to remarks like that, and being laughed at, but I really didn't need it tonight. Hanging out with Dare hasn't been as awkward as I'd feared. I'd kind of forgotten to be worried about how I look. Now, I feel self-conscious about facing him again, but there's no hope for it. Surely, he's realized by now I'm not going to try to get with him or anything, and we can continue the friendship.

We've run out of candy. I hang a note on the door so no one else will knock, and reluctantly return to the living room.

Dare stands by my couch, and I'm struck again by how gorgeous he is. The muscles in his back bulge and flex as he removes his tie and rolls up his sleeves. I'm frozen in place, watching him when he turns, and a smirk lifts his lips. "You're checking me out."

My face instantly heats, and I roll my eyes. "No, I'm not. I was just wondering why you're wearing a suit."

The mirth leaves his eyes. "I had to go to a funeral today. A friend of mine died of a heart attack."

"Oh, I'm sorry."

"It's okay. Jed and I weren't close, but I had to go pay my respects." He looks at me. "My friend, Justus, was close to him. We all went out to drink in his memory last night. I don't usually get trashed like that."

"I'm surprised you remember last night," I tease.

"Oh, I remember."

The weight behind those words isn't something I'm going to address or question. Finally, we settle down to watch the movie.

CHAPTER
FOUR

DARE

All I want to do is strip Ayda naked and fuck her until she can't remember anything except my name, but I can't treat her the way I've treated other women. She's different, and I want more from her than I've ever wanted from a woman. All I've ever been interested in is sex, but something about this woman makes me want more.

I enjoy being with her like this, sprawled on the couch watching horror movies and eating leftover Halloween candy. She seemed nervous when I first arrived, but it didn't take her long to warm up to me again. Well, somewhat.

We sit on her couch, but she's careful to keep her distance, like she doesn't want to touch me. The expression on her face betrays what she really feels. I've pretended not to notice her furtive glances, but I'm not keeping up the charade much longer.

When the movie ends, she goes to the kitchen, calling back over her shoulder. "Would you like something to drink?"

I know what I'd like and it's time to claim it. Her back is to me while she peruses the fridge, and she gasps when she steps backward right into my chest. I wrap my arm around her waist, my hand splaying across her stomach, and pull her against me.

"What are you doing?" Her voice is faint, like maybe she doesn't really want an answer to that question.

"Touching you," I reply, my lips against her ear. Her shiver makes me smile. "I couldn't resist anymore."

She relaxes in my arms, breathing a small sigh as I run my lips down the smooth skin of her neck. Her hands land on my chest when I spin her to face me, but she keeps her head down. "Look at me, beautiful."

She flinches at the word beautiful, and her body stiffens, but she reluctantly meets my gaze. I can feel her trying to withdraw, trying to take control. It isn't going to happen. Grabbing her hips and backing her against the kitchen counter, I catch her soft lips with mine.

A woman told me once that a first kiss should be soft, polite even, but I'm not polite, and my need for her takes over. Her lips part under mine, and I take complete advantage of the opportunity, plunging my tongue inside to taste her soft mouth. Her hand jumps to my hair, gripping it as she tilts her head and kisses me harder, a small groan rumbling her throat.

The sound goes straight to my cock, making it strain against my zipper. Though I've gotten a taste of her smart ass attitude through the wall, in person she comes off as shy and timid, but not one ounce of that is who she truly is. That's clear in the way she tugs my hair, her hand squeezing my ass while we basically maul each other in her kitchen.

Another moan leaves her lips when she presses against me, my thigh rubbing between her legs. I can feel her heat through her thin shorts. It's driving me out of my mind. Spinning her around so her back is to me again, I slide my hand under her shirt onto the warm skin of her stomach.

"Dare," she breathes, when my fingers travel under the waistband of her shorts and panties.

"I'm going to make you come now, Ayda."

My hand slides lower, until I can feel the effect my words have on her. She likes the dirty talk. "Put your hands around my neck, baby, and keep them there."

She complies without hesitation, and the arch in her back pushes her tits out. I cup her breast with one hand and run my thumb over her nipple, loving how it stiffens when I roll it between my fingers. Her head lies back against my chest, and her arms are clamped tightly around my neck as I slide a thick finger inside her.

I swear the sounds she makes while I finger her will play in my head forever. She twists in my arms, growing wetter by the second. When I bend my finger to find just the right spot inside her, she gasps, lets go of my neck, and reaches for the edge of the counter.

"Get those arms back up," I growl, pinching her nipple. She quickly obeys, fisting a handful of my hair. Christ, submissive and wild. This woman will be the death of me.

She squirms, trying to stay on her feet while the sensations grow stronger, my thumb on her clit bringing her right to the edge. "That's right, baby. Come for me," I whisper into her ear when she starts to contract around my finger. A second later, she comes on my hand, her soft cry filling the room. It's the sexiest fucking thing I've ever seen.

Her hands fall to the counter while she catches her breath, and I kiss up the side of her neck. As soon as my lips approach her scarred skin, she steps away, cursing. Was her scar the reason she wouldn't agree to meet me all this time? "It's okay," I tell her.

"You should go," she says, putting even more distance between us before I can further reassure her. "I didn't mean to lead you on or make you think we were going to fuck."

She won't look at me, but she doesn't jerk away when I pull her close again. "We're going to do so much more than fuck, Ayda."

A loud pounding echoes through the room and she jumps, backing away from me.

"Dare, damn it! Open up," Justus yells. Christ, he's going to knock my door down banging on it like that, loud enough to be heard from Ayda's place. What the hell is going on now?

"Give me a minute," I tell Ayda, doing my best not to be pissed at Justus for breaking the moment. I'm sure this has to do with Jed.

She doesn't answer, but follows me to the door. Justus is leaning against my door when I step outside. "There you are!" He waves his hand in my direction. "I can't stay there, man. We have to get someone else. I feel like he's fucking haunting me."

Shit. I toss him my keys. "Go on in. I'll be there in a second."

Without waiting for a response, I turn to face Ayda. "That's Justus. He's having a hard time with Jed's death."

Relief washes over her features. "Go take care of your friend."

My fingers brush her hair back from her eyes. "Are you okay?"

A fake smile jumps across her face. "I'm fine. Really, go see what's wrong with him."

Torn, I hesitate for a moment before nodding. "I'll talk to you later."

"Sure." It's clear she can't wait for me to leave. As badly as I want to stay and smooth things over, I need to see what's up with Justus. He's not the most stable guy when he isn't upset.

I plant one more kiss on her soft lips before she closes the door behind me.

Justus stands at my kitchen counter, pouring a shot of whiskey from the bottle I always keep in the cabinet. "Dude, are you finally nailing the neighbor girl instead of eavesdropping on her?"

"No." I grab the bottle from his hand and take a drink. Something tells me I'm going to need it. "And keep your voice down. We can hear through these walls. Do you want to tell me what's going on?"

He sighs, and shuffles his feet, his ears glowing red while he stares at the counter. "I know I said I'd stay at the farm, but I can't. It's fucking creepy. Seriously, you wouldn't believe the noises I heard. I think the bastard is haunting the place."

Trying not to smile, I ask, "Have you ever spent the night in the country?"

"I've spent a few nights in that house with Jed." He slides the shot glass toward me, and I refill it. "It doesn't matter. It won't work in the long run anyway. Over an hour and a half commute to work and to ISH? We have to find someone else."

I have someone in mind to take Jed's place, but it's risky. We'll have to let another person in on the secret of what we do. How many people are going to be okay not only with us killing an abuser, but also with living on the property where we dispose of the remains?

"I have someone in mind," I reveal.

Justus looks up with a mixture of relief and curiosity. "Yeah? Who?"

My mind wanders back to my last conversation with Tucker. Since I brought him the burger the first time, I've made a habit of grabbing him something whenever I stop for dinner. We usually sit on the curb to eat, and last time was no exception.

"Don't you get disability or a pension or something from the military?" I asked him.

"Not when you're dishonorably discharged and court martialed."

Silence descended for a few moments before I volunteered, "I've done time, too. State prison."

"Yeah? How long?"

"Three years."

"Four," he said, tossing a burnt French fry aside.

"You win."

He frowned, staring in the distance. "Pretty sure we both lost."

"It's taking me a while to bounce back."

"What were you in for?"

"Aggravated assault. I beat my sister's abuser half to death. Put the fucker in a wheelchair."

He looked at me like he was seeing me for the first time. "No shit? Your sister okay?"

"She's doing good. Going to college."

"Worth it then," he mumbled.

"I wouldn't do it differently if I had the chance."

We chewed in silence, ignoring the curious glances from the neighbors making their way to their doors. I was a second away from asking him what got him locked up when he balled up his hamburger wrapper and volunteered the information. "Involuntary manslaughter."

Damn. "Here or when you were deployed?"

"Afghanistan. I shot a man in my unit. He was raping a young Afghani girl."

"And they locked you up for that?" Shit, wasn't there a law in place if you were defending someone else?

He scoffed and got to his feet. "I shot one of our own over what they considered an NHI attack."

"NHI?"

"No humans involved."

"That's fucked up."

Shaking his head, he laughed bitterly. "Everything is fucked up."

Justus is staring at me, and I realize I never answered his question. "Let me talk to him first."

———

Tucker agrees to come inside for a beer when I find him leaning against the fence that surrounds the now empty pool. Justus decided to go to Landon's, where we recently moved ISH headquarters, so Tucker and I have my place to ourselves.

He looks uncomfortable sitting on the edge of my couch, so I get right to the point. "I have a proposition for you, if you're interested. A job and a place to stay."

His gaze is wary. "I'm listening."

"Let me ask you a question first. The man you killed for raping a girl. If you had the chance to go back, would you do it again?"

"Yes," he replies instantly. "There's right and there's wrong, but the government doesn't always see it that way."

"I agree. I work with a group who track down pedophiles and online predators. Most of the time, we report them to the cops—anonymously—but occasionally we find an asshole who keeps beating the system. I'm talking about the fucking scum of the earth. Men who abuse and sexually molest children, sometimes buy and sell them into sexual slavery. Those don't get reported. We make them disappear."

He scowls. "And you think because I've killed before, I might want to be what...a hit man for you?"

"No. No killing. We own a property outside the city, about an hour and a half away. It's a farmhouse with a couple hundred acres, most of it woods. Our friend who was taking care of the place just died, and we need someone who's willing to live there, keep the place up."

"What's the catch?"

"There's risk involved, I'm not going to lie. We

dispose of the bodies there, and if it's ever discovered, you'd be an accessory at the least."

His hands run through his overlong oily hair. "You bury them there?"

"Not exactly. Bodies are too easy to dig up. We want to leave the least amount of evidence behind as possible. If you decide to live there, you'll need to take care of a few pigs. Feed them, clean up shit, et cetera. Oh, and take care of Humper." I wave my hand. "We'll pay all the bills, plus hook you up with cash every month."

"Humper?"

"He was Jed's dog."

Tucker's eyes meet mine. "I'd need a car."

"There's a truck on the property. You're welcome to it. Look, why don't we drive out there tomorrow and you can see if you're interested?"

He thinks about it for a long second before nodding. "I can do that."

"Great, you can crash on the couch here tonight if you want."

Getting to his feet, he shakes his head. "No thanks. Just come grab me when you want to go."

He lets himself out, and I breathe a sigh of relief. That could've gone either way. He could've been horrified and called the police, but since he's stepped outside the law himself to right a wrong, I figured he was a safe bet. Now I have to convince him to join us.

What a fucking day. A funeral, and an evening with Ayda. An end and a new beginning. Hopefully.

CHAPTER
FIVE

AYDA

My weak legs barely carry me to the couch before they give out, and I flop onto the cushion, my brain spinning while I struggle to figure out what the hell just happened. My gaze travels to the kitchen where Dare had his hand down my shorts, and my cheeks burn. Christ, the man is a walking wet dream, and I made out with him. Who am I kidding? I'm pretty sure when you come all over a guy's hand, you've gone beyond making out.

I never dreamed he'd try anything with me, and I didn't mean to let it happen. From the second he wrapped those strong arms around me, I never had a chance of resisting. His hands are so big, his touch rough and mind blowing. I've never had anyone just grab me like that and I came as much from his commanding attitude as I did from his fingers inside me.

For a few moments, I forgot everything. My world narrowed to the sensation of his warm, hard body wrapped around mine. The man could make me forget my own name. And he only touched me. What would sex with him be like? A thrill courses through me at the thought of him completely naked, his skin slick with sweat, muscles flexing as he takes me hard and fast.

I'd adjusted to not having a sex life. Other than an occasional stress relief session with my vibrator, I didn't think much about it. Five minutes with Dare and I feel like a wanton slut, ready to beg for it.

It wasn't until he almost brought his lips to my face that reality set in. I don't know if he got carried away or maybe had his eyes closed while he kissed my neck, but I couldn't stand the thought of his mouth landing on that puckered skin. The revulsion he was sure to feel, even if he hid it well. Thank goodness his friend showed up when he did.

I can't bear to go to my room where I might hear him. The couch is a better option. With a blanket wrapped around me and a throw pillow tucked under my cheek, it's comfortable enough. I just want to sleep and pretend this never happened. Apparently, pleasure given by a Greek God of a man after years of only self-induced orgasms knocks you out, because I'm asleep in seconds.

The beep of my cell alerting me I have a voicemail wakes me the next morning. Groggy, I sit up on the couch, shaking off a dream I can't recall, but I know included a lot of naked, muscled skin. Damn it, I can't even escape Dare in my dreams.

Lisa's voice rings out when I play back my messages, asking if I can meet with her student, Ryan, this afternoon at one. It's nearly eleven o'clock, so I shoot her a quick text, letting her know I'll be there, then jump in the shower.

My reflection in the bathroom mirror makes me pause. There's a pink spot on my neck. A hickey. He gave me a damn hickey. I should be annoyed, but seeing it only reminds me of his lips on my neck, the heat of his body, how amazing he smelled.

What has happened to my life in the past few days? I'd normally spend the day working on a design project, reading, watching TV, then maybe dancing alone in the evening. How did I end up here, rubbing makeup over a hickey before heading to teach at a dance school?

Traffic is light, and I end up pulling in the lot of the studio in plenty of time. Lisa greets me when I walk into the lobby. "Ayda, glad you could make it. Ryan's very excited to get a new routine." She waves to a blond headed boy down the hall. He grins, practically running to meet us. Ryan is twelve years old, but small for his age, with a thin body clearly sculpted by years of dance.

"Ryan, this is Ms. Brooks," she introduces us.

"Nice to meet you," he says with a shy smile.

"It's nice to meet you, too."

Lisa lays a hand on Ryan's shoulder. "You can use the purple room. It's empty until three." While her advanced classes take place in the main studio, Lisa has two other rooms where she holds the smaller classes for the youngest children. She turns to me. "Come find me if you need me."

I give Ryan a reassuring smile. "I'm going to change, then I'll meet you there. Why don't you run through the warm up exercises?"

"Sure." He heads down the hall, and Lisa looks at me.

"Thank you for helping him. If you have any issues, I'll be in the office."

"We'll be fine," I assure her. I can feel the eyes on me when I walk back to the dressing room. A young, pretty woman teaches a group of five and six-year-olds in one room, while a teenage couple practice a routine on the main floor. I'm sure they're curious who I am, since I've never been here when the school is open.

I change quickly and join Ryan at the barre to warm up. "Have you heard the song you'll be performing to?" I ask him.

"Yeah, I love it. Lisa sent me the title last night, and I think I drove my dad crazy playing it over and over."

He smiles when I laugh. When our muscles are sufficiently warm and limber, we get started. I'm blown away by this young boy's skill and determination. Lisa is right. He feels the music, bringing a passion to dance most boys his age aren't capable of. It isn't until we hear his father's voice nearly two hours later, that we fall to the floor, sweating and breathing hard.

"Sorry to interrupt," his dad says, "but Ryan has a birthday party to get to this afternoon." He's not what I'd expect a dance dad to look like. Big, bearded, and burly. He approaches me with a wide smile. "You must be Ms. Brooks. I'm Kevin." His eyes land for a moment on the scar on my face, but it doesn't bother me. He isn't staring, and it's actually weirder sometimes when people go out of their way *not* to look.

"Please, call me Ayda. You have a very talented young man here."

"Yes, I do. Although, he could smell a little better," he

teases, and Ryan tries to wipe his sweaty head on his dad's shirt.

Laughing, I tell Ryan, "You did a great job. Lisa will let you know when our next practice session will be."

"Great! Bye Ms. Brooks!" he calls, and I hear him tell his dad as they're leaving, "You have to see this routine. It's awesome. I'm going to win."

Lisa catches me on my way out. "Ryan's excited. I guess the lesson went well?"

"He's a quick study."

"Yes, he is. Would you be willing to work with him once a week until the competition?"

Pausing, I consider her offer. To my surprise, I had fun today. I expected to be preoccupied by the stares and whispers surrounding me, not just because of my scar, but because of my name. At one time, I was an up-and-coming ballerina, destined for stardom. A fall from that sort of height is news by itself, never mind the awful circumstances which caused it. I'm thrilled no one recognized me.

"Sure. Just let me know what day."

"I'll text you," she promises, and flashes a smile before heading to teach her next class.

Maybe it's because I managed a day in public without wanting to crawl under a rock somewhere, but I decide I'm not ready to go home. It's getting cooler by the day and I need to shop for some new winter clothes.

Sadie picks up the phone on the first ring. "Hey, woman. Are you still working?" I ask, unlocking my car.

"Nope. Had an early day. What are you doing?"

"I was thinking about heading to the mall. Do you want to meet me?"

The pause in her response is long enough to make me wonder if the call dropped. "You want to go to the mall? Voluntarily?"

"I need some clothes, and I'm starving. I want one of those giant cinnamon rolls from the food court. Do you want to come?"

"Absolutely, I just had to peek out the window, see if there were any flying pigs in the area. Meet you there in twenty?"

"Very funny, bitch. I'll be by the north entrance."

Sadie bounds up to me a few minutes later, her blond hair whipping in the wind, and links her arm through mine, leading us inside. "Does this guy you're 'sort of' talking to have anything to do with why you're suddenly willing to shop in the middle of the afternoon?"

"No, that's no big deal, I told you."

"Have you actually met him face to face yet?" she asks, while we grab our cinnamon rolls and sit at a nearby table.

"Uh...yeah. He brought me dinner."

I stop there, but I know Sadie will never let me off that easy. "And?"

"And he kissed me," I admit, feeling my cheeks warm up when I recall what the kiss lead to.

Nearby customers glance in our direction when she squeals. "You slept with him!"

"Sadie! Shut up!" Christ, tell the whole mall. "I didn't sleep with him. We just...I mean...he just," I stumble over the words, finally leaning toward her to whisper. "We made out, and he fingered me, okay?"

Her smile is wide and mischievous. "I'll bet it was

way better than okay. Damn girl, he's a pile of sexy. Did you, you know, return the favor?"

"No."

"Why the hell not?" She pops a chunk of cinnamon roll into her mouth.

"His friend showed up."

"Cockblocked. That sucks. When are you going to see him again? We should go to the spa, get you a wax, do our nails, the works."

I knew Sadie would run with the information. I love how excited she gets, it's part of what makes hanging out with her so fun, but I don't want her to get carried away. "I don't think I'll be seeing him again."

"What, why not?"

"We're too different." I shrug, keeping my eyes pointed at the shoppers flowing by.

Sadie sighs and shakes her head. "Bullshit. You're making excuses. You're scared."

Damn it. Can't put anything past her. "He didn't see me naked. He slid his hand down my shorts. Once he sees me, it won't go well. I'd rather have a good memory of him, and maybe be able to keep talking to him occasionally."

"Just because one asshole was too blind to see what you have to offer doesn't mean they'll all react that way."

Rationally, I know she's right, but she has no idea how it feels. The only guy I dated after my injuries showed me exactly what to expect. His name was Lawrence, and we met a few weeks after I was released from the hospital. Back when I still bothered to wear makeup, spending hours finding the best way to cover the facial scars as completely as possible.

They were still discernible, but not as instantly visible as they are without makeup. We dated for a few weeks, and everything was good until the first night I brought him home with me. No amount of concealer can cover the marred skin that runs down my right arm and covers my ribs on that side. Luckily, my neck escaped damage, but my right shoulder bears skin that's crumpled and misshapen.

I knew before we even finished fucking that he was done. I didn't miss the way he winced when he saw me bare. His eyes were closed most of the time and he was careful not to touch me anywhere near the scarred tissue. Blurting a lame excuse about having to work early the next morning, he couldn't get away from me fast enough after we were done. I never heard from him again.

That was when I knew I had to accept the harsh reality. This is my life. I'm lucky to be alive, and generally healthy, but some things are always going to be off limits to me. Sex is one of them. Oh, I'm aware there are guys out there who would still fuck me. Let's be honest, most men will fuck anything with a pulse and a wet spot, but I can't stand to have sex knowing the guy is disgusted. Or has some deformity fetish.

"I know," I answer Sadie, tucking my hair behind my ear. "But have you seen this guy?"

"Yes, and that's why I know you need to climb him like a tree."

Laughing, I take the last drink of my soda. "You're crazy. Now, let's go spend some money. My jeans don't fit, and I'm tired of pulling them up."

"Skinny ass."

"Jumbo tits."

"Don't hate," she giggles, and we head for the department store.

———

It's late when I get home and I'm relieved when I make it inside without running into Dare. I'm not ready to face him yet. His apartment has been quiet, so I assume he's not home when I crawl into bed, but his deep voice travels through the wall seconds after I lie down.

"What are you wearing?"

Maybe if I ignore him, he'll get the message.

"Hmm...no answer. Maybe you're naked."

Shoving the pillow over my head, I try to block him out.

"If you don't answer me, I'm going to assume you're naked. No wait. You're naked except for the whipped cream."

Now, I'm fighting the urge to laugh.

"I can't be ignored, Ayda. I know lots of annoying songs. I'll sing until you answer me."

There's no way I'm answering now. I want to see if he'll actually sing.

"Okay, babe. You're forcing me to do this," he warns, amusement thick in his voice.

I expected a rendition of one-hundred bottles of beer on the wall or something similar. The unexpected sound of Rebecca Black's *Friday* catches me off guard. I'm sure he can hear me laughing as he runs through the whole song and then begins again. How long will he keep it up?

"Okay, shut up!" I laugh, when he begins again for the fourth time.

"Well?" he asks.

"Well, what?"

"Are you wearing only whipped cream?"

Smiling, I pull my comforter to my neck. "Of course, that's what I always wear to bed. Plus a couple of chocolate kisses."

"I'm coming over."

I can't tell if he's serious or still screwing with me. "No!"

"Why not?"

"I'm exhausted. I'm going to sleep."

His bed creaks, and I picture him rolling over. His ass looked amazing in those boxer briefs and my mind conjures an idea of how it'd look bare. "Did you work today? What do you do?"

"No, I didn't work today. I'm a graphic designer, and I dabble in marketing a bit." My curiosity outweighs my desire not to encourage him. "What do you do?"

"I'm a hacker."

Again, I have no idea if he's serious. "Should I worry about my bank account and change all my passwords?"

He chuckles, and I picture his smile. It's not fair for a man who looks like him to also have the sexiest smile I've ever seen. "Your accounts are safe. I work in cyber security."

"You work from home?" I ask, surprised we may have that in common.

"Sometimes. Depends on what I'm working on." He's vague, and his tone shows me he doesn't want to elaborate even before he changes the subject. "What did you do today?"

"A friend of mine asked me to come in and teach a dance routine to one of her students, then I hung out with a friend."

"You dance? What style?"

"I used to dance ballet, but the dance we're working on is contemporary. Her student has a competition coming and needed some help."

"A dancer," he groans. "That explains your tight little body. How am I supposed to sleep now? All I can picture is you in only a tutu."

Hearing him describe my body is bittersweet. I do have a well-toned dancer's figure, but it's not what he's picturing. "I don't wear a tutu."

"In my spank bank, you do."

"Oh my god. You didn't just say that."

"Naked in a tutu, moaning for me when you come, just like last night."

I'm so torn. Part of me wants to go over there, strip naked and ride him like a two humped camel out of Egypt, but I can't. I don't want to see the revulsion on his face when his fantasy dancer turns out to have a body like Freddy Krueger. "I'm going to sleep now."

"Don't be embarrassed. It was hot as hell. Next time, I want to hear you scream my name."

"There won't be a next time."

"Like hell there won't."

"Good night, Dare."

"Good night, Ayda."

CHAPTER
SIX

DARE

"Are you sure about this guy?" Landon asks. All the members of ISH are gathered at our new headquarters, and I've spent the last few minutes vouching for Tucker. Justus and Jeremy are on board, but Landon is a bit skeptical.

"As sure as anyone can be. He's killed to protect a woman. He's not going to turn us in for protecting children. Also, he was a soldier. He knows how to handle himself."

Landon's girlfriend, Zoe, cuddles up to his side. She's the only one outside of our group who knows what we do. We intervened when her brother's boyfriend was being abused. I never thought Landon would settle down with a woman, but watching him with Zoe makes me think of Ayda.

There's a lot she doesn't know about me, and though

I want to get to know her—and fuck her brains out—I'm afraid to let her get too close or learn too much. She's sweet and kind. I doubt a criminal ex-con would be her type.

I finally get a reluctant nod from Landon and he asks, "Do you want me to go with you when you take Tucker out to the farm?"

His gaze travels to Zoe then back to me, and I know he's hoping I'll pass on that offer. He tries to spend every minute with that girl. Don't get me wrong, Zoe is great. She has no problem hanging out and she can throw our bullshit back at us without hesitation. I'm happy for Landon, even though it means we don't get to hit the bars like we used to.

"No offense, but I'd rather take him in the daylight."

"Poor raisin," Justus teases, faking a mournful tone. He's joking around like usual, but I know Jed is still on his mind.

"Fuck off, stripper," Landon replies, slinging his arm around Zoe. Landon and I have been friends since we were kids. He has a genetic disease that prevents him from going outside in the daytime. The smallest amount of sunlight leaves him with severe burns and a high risk for skin cancers.

"I'll go if you want. I've got nothing going on today," Jeremy volunteers. "We can hang out and drink a few beers, get to know the guy."

"Sounds good. Meet me out there about four?"

"I'll be there."

I turn to Landon. "Justus told me about the new forum. You think you've discovered a trafficking ring?"

"Looks that way, but we need a lot more info. If it is a

ring, they cover their tracks well. I hacked in and lurked last night. Lots of talk about seasoning a new addition who got caught reckless eyeballing."

Fuck. Seasoning is synonymous with torture, both mental and physical, to get the victim to obey with questioning. Victims are instructed to keep their eyes on the ground. If they make eye contact with another pimp, they can become his property. Crazy shit.

"Do you need me back here tonight?"

"Nah, get the new guy settled. I'll catch you up tomorrow if there's any news."

Tucker sits under a tree across from my apartment when I return, and he hops in my passenger seat after I wave him over. Our first stop is a gas station to fill the tank and grab a twelve pack of beer. "My buddy Jeremy is going to meet us there. He works with ISH as well."

"How many are in your group?" Tucker asks, while I pull back onto the highway.

"Four. I'll take you to meet Landon another night. He has a genetic disorder and has to stay out of the sunlight. Plus, he has a new girlfriend."

Tucker laughs and nods. "Nothing makes a guy go MIA faster."

"She's cool, though. She also knows what we do, but she's the only one outside of the group."

Tucker eyes me for a few moments. "Are you seeing Ayda?"

I guess I shouldn't be surprised he noticed since he spends a lot of time in the parking lot. "We're hanging out." If you can count talking through a wall as hanging out.

"She's a good girl. Had a hard way to go. She's not

exactly the type you only hang out with." There's a warning in his voice. "Are you trying to hook up with her?"

"No."

He shakes his head. "I don't want to see her get jerked around."

It figures the first time I'm actually interested in getting to know a woman and even having a relationship, I get accused of being an asshole. "I'm trying to get to know her, but she doesn't make it easy."

"She's a stubborn one," he agrees, laughing.

A light rain begins to fall when I park outside the farmhouse and lead Tucker to the barn. "Pigs are the only animals we keep. There's pig feed in those storage bins. Be sure to keep them closed tight or the mice and raccoons will tear it up. Just dump in five pounds of feed each morning and shovel out the shit. There's a compost heap near the tree line where you can dump it."

"Seems easy enough," Tucker grunts. His eyes meet mine, shining with a fierce intelligence. I haven't been so closely scrutinized since I was in a courtroom. "Now, do you want to explain why you keep pigs?"

Nodding, I lead him around to the back where the industrial wood chipper is stored. "The bodies of the perverts get run through here, then dumped into the trough for the pigs to eat."

The only perceptible response is a slight stiffening of his spine. "And am I responsible for that?"

"No. As I said, all you need to do is feed the pigs, keep the place up, grass mowed, et cetera. If we need the chipper, one of us will call. Most likely in the middle of the night. We'll take care of the body, then bleach the trough and chipper to make sure there's nothing left. You never have to take part or witness any of it."

He stares at the chipper silently, and the rain starts to pick up. "You can still say no if this isn't for you. No harm, no foul."

He blinks as if he's just awakened or maybe walked out of a dark theater. "I'm good. I mean, I can do it. No problem."

"Great. I'll show you the house."

A tour doesn't take long, and we're returning to the living room when Jeremy walks in holding a twelve pack. Tucker sticks out his hand before I can introduce him. "Tucker Long."

"Jeremy Martin, nice to meet you, man."

"Same goes."

Jeremy glances around. "It's weird without Jed here, isn't it?"

"Justus couldn't stand to stay here, especially alone. He was pretty close to Jed," I explain to Tucker.

Jeremy flops into a chair and opens a beer. Tucker and I follow suit. "I didn't know Jed all that well, but he was a good guy," Jeremy says.

"He was," I agree. "And a horny old fucker, too. Quite a few times when Justus and I would show up, he'd have a woman waiting for him upstairs. Said he met them at bingo, of all places."

Jeremy snorts, "I can't picture his big, bearded ass playing bingo."

There's a brief knock at the door and we hear Justus call out, "It's me, assholes!" He appears in the living room carrying beer. His face darkens when he glances around the living room, and I know he's thinking of all the times he hung out with Jed here.

Justus has never had a family. He grew up in a series of foster homes, and Jed became a father figure to him. "Tucker, this is Justus." I nod toward him as he takes a seat on the couch.

"Nice to meet you. Have you decided if you're going to stay?" Justus asks.

Tucker leans back, resting his foot on his knee. "Yes. I'll take good care of the place."

Justus eyes him. "You're about Jed's size. There's a closet and dresser full of clothes in the bedroom upstairs. I was going to donate them, but you're welcome to them."

"Thanks." Tucker's response is clipped, but not rude. No man wants to accept charity. None of us see it that way, but I'm sure that's how this job and house offer feels to Tucker.

"We were just telling Tucker about Jed and his bingo women," I announce, changing the subject.

Justus laughs and we start trading stories and experiences we shared with Jed. A few hours later, we're all nicely lit. Justus pops open another beer and continues, "We were in line at the dollar store and the woman in front of us was wearing a skin tight tank top with no bra. She had nipples you could key a car with, and the woman in the next aisle was shooting her shitty looks. She mumbled an insult. All I caught was the word 'slut' but the woman in front of us heard it and her face turned red.

"She looked desperate to get out of there, but the cashier was taking his time. And I swear, Jed looked her right in the eye and said, 'Ain't nothing wrong with showing a little nipple. Without them, titties wouldn't have a point.'

"The woman laughed despite her embarrassment, and the judgmental bitch in the next aisle huffed away. 'Don't worry about her, honey,' Jed told her. 'It's just jealousy. She was so ugly she'd make a freight train take a dirt road.' The next time I came over, she was in his bed."

Everyone laughs, and Justus has a real smile on his face for the first time in days. "To Jed," Tucker says, holding up his beer. "I'm sorry I didn't know him."

"To Jed," we chorus.

Tucker looks around the group. "I have to ask how you get away with what you do. Don't the police notice missing pedophiles?"

I nod at Jeremy, who explains, "Most of the time we report them to the police, anonymously. We gather all the information we can, screenshots of online conversations, IP addresses, et cetera. There's a task force in Indy that deals with online predators and human trafficking, and they've never failed to use what we send them to lock up the sickos. When they drop the ball, we pick it up, and turn the sick fuck into pig food. There have been a couple of missing person reports in the past, but nothing has ever been traced back to us. These guys have usually alienated any family or friends long before we ever get involved.

"When we do need help from the authorities, we have a contact in another group called Striking Back. They help women and children who are victims of domestic violence, and have a lot of friends in high places, including judges, FBI agents, and cops. The Reed brothers aren't guys you want to mess with. It's good they're on our side."

"I'll introduce you to Mason Reed," I promise. "His contact number is listed in the cell I gave you as an emergency number. If anything ever happens and you can't reach one of us, he's the one to go to."

It falls silent for a few minutes before Jeremy asks me, "What's up with the chick next door to you? Are you fucking her?"

Thank you, Landon, for having such a huge mouth.

"No, I'm not fucking her."

"But you want to," Justus pursues.

Tucker stares at me while I answer. "I'm trying to get to know her. She's kind of skittish."

"Any idea what happened to her?"

"No," I reply, at the same time Tucker says, "Acid."

My head whips around. "What?"

"She had acid thrown on her when she was young. I don't know the circumstances, but she told me that much."

Fuck. I imagined it was a car accident or something, not an assault. "You don't know who?"

"I didn't ask, and she didn't say."

"I'll kill the motherfucker," I growl.

The smiles exchanged between Justus and Jeremy don't escape my attention, but I ignore them.

We drink until the beer runs dry, and Tucker eventually goes to crash upstairs. As dawn approaches, Jeremy takes one of the other two guest rooms, leaving me and Justus on the front porch. The horizon glows pink with wispy clouds strewn through the sky.

Justus stares into the distance. "Jed would like Tucker.

I think he'll work out fine."

———

Ayda has been avoiding me and only giving short, clipped answers when I try to talk to her through the wall. It's starting to piss me off. After her reaction to me in her kitchen, I know she feels the same pull I do between us. I'm not going to let her ignore it.

The faint sounds of her TV permeate the wall, like she's trying to keep it down, so I don't know she's there. "What are you watching?" I ask.

After a few seconds of silence, she replies, "The news."

"Thanksgiving is a few days away."

"Yep."

"Do you go to your family, or do you cook?"

A thump and a sigh make me picture her slumped against the wall. "Neither. I skip it."

She plans to spend Thanksgiving alone? That's not happening. "You're coming with me. My friend's girl-friend is cooking at his house and we're invited."

"You mean you're invited," she snorts.

"Me and whoever the hell I want to bring. Be ready about noon."

"Thanks for the invitation, Dare, but I'll have to pass." My cock hardens when she says my name, which is fucking ridiculous.

"You don't have to bring anything. I'll stop and grab a pie or something."

"I said no."

"I heard you. You're in a mood today." She's usually

full of smart ass retorts. "What's wrong?"

It's quiet for a long moment before she replies. "You know the man who sleeps behind the dumpster? I bring him food sometimes, but he hasn't been there the past few days. I think something might've happened to him."

Damn it. I should've realized she'd be worried about him. "He's fine. A friend of mine owns a farm and needed some help. He gave him a job and a place to stay."

"Really? How do you know him?"

"Same way you do. We've spent a few dinners together on the curb."

Silence stretches out, and I can almost hear the gears whirring in her brain. "Thank you for helping him. I tried, but he wouldn't go to a shelter or anything."

"He's really fond of you. I invited him for Thanksgiving dinner as well, but he said he's going to visit family."

"Why the hell was he on the street if he has family?"

The indignation in her voice makes me smile. "He might be full of shit and just doesn't want to come."

"So, you'll take no for an answer from him?"

"He's not as sexy as you."

"You're so full of shit, I'll bet your eyes are brown."

"They're blue, actually. I'm surprised you didn't notice. They're pretty sexy too."

"You're so conceited," she laughs.

"I'm not conceited, sweetheart. I'm confident. I'll pick you up at noon."

"Fine, but I'll make the pie." She yawns, and I hear her TV click off. "Good night, Dare."

"Good night, Ayda."

CHAPTER
SEVEN

AYDA

I can't believe I agreed to go with Dare to a Thanksgiving dinner. I've managed not to meet him face to face since Halloween, but when he told me what he did for Tucker, I couldn't say no. My hands shake with nerves as I straighten my hair, then pull on jeans and a sweater. I have no idea who will be at the dinner, and meeting new people always makes me want to throw up. The inevitable stares and whispers. Even blatant questions about my scars from those who seem to think it'd make a good conversation starter.

He knocks on the door a few minutes before noon, and the sight of him steals the oxygen from my brain. His midnight blue Henley shirt brings out the color of his eyes and clings to his torso, showing off his defined chest and abs. Dark jeans hug his ass, and I may have a slight urge to squeeze it. Just a little.

His gaze sweeps down to my feet and up again until his eyes meet mine, making my heart leap forward. He leans to place a soft kiss below my ear and says, "You look good enough to eat."

"Then maybe we can skip this whole Thanksgiving thing," I suggest. I'm not completely joking. I'd much rather spend the day alone with him, but he won't let me get away with it.

Chuckling, he steps inside. "No way, babe. I want to introduce you to my friends." He sniffs. "It smells fantastic in here. Apple pie?"

"And cherry. I figured chances are someone will have brought pumpkin."

I pull the two pies from the fridge, and he takes them from me, balancing them on one huge palm while we walk to the parking lot. An icy breeze cuts through my clothes like they're made of paper, and it's a relief to settle into his warm SUV.

"Are there going to be a lot of people there?" I ask, trying not to sound as concerned as I am.

"Let's see, my friends Landon, Justus, and Jeremy. Landon's girlfriend, Zoe, and her brother, Ethan. I think maybe Ethan's boyfriend. I can't remember his name." He tilts his head and knocks me out with that killer smile. "You'll like Zoe. She's a smart ass too."

"Too?" I smack him on the shoulder, grinning.

"I stand by my statement."

Landon's house is huge. Add on a few rooms and you could call it a mansion. I wonder what he does for a living. I don't have much time to dwell on it before I'm led into a large, bright kitchen crammed full of hot guys.

Seriously, it's like they were plucked from a sexy, bad boy warehouse.

"Ayda, this is Landon, Jeremy, and Justus," Dare announces, gesturing to each as he says their name while keeping his arm around my shoulders. "Be nice, assholes."

Landon and Dare could be brothers with their dark hair and blue eyes, although Landon's look a bit green, and Dare's body is way bulkier. Justus is hot with his blond curls and a dimple that shows when he smiles at me. Jeremy is more classically handsome with clean cut, brown hair and a lean body.

After the introductions are out of the way, Zoe kicks everyone out of the kitchen. It may have had something to do with Dare knocking a bowl of flour to the floor. "All right! Everyone with a penis, out!" she exclaims, then turns to me. "Stay and chat, Ayda, if you'd like to get away from these brutes for a bit."

Landon grabs her around the waist and whispers something in her ear while Dare looks down at me. "Are you okay?"

He's asking if I'm okay without him, and while I want to follow him, I don't want to be the clingy girl. Besides, Zoe seems nice. At least it's a lot quieter once the crowd of sexy moves to the living room.

"What can I help with?" I ask, hopping onto a stool. Zoe smiles and shoves a cutting board full of celery and onions toward me.

"Would you mind chopping them?" She pours a glass of wine and hands it to me. "Trust me, you'll need it. We're drowning in testosterone tonight. Six guys and us."

Laughing, I accept and start chopping the vegetables.

"How did you and Dare meet?"

"He lives next door to me. How did you meet Landon?" I ask, trying to steer the conversation away from me.

"I met him at a club the first time, but I didn't get to know him until later when I answered an ad for a housekeeper." She gestures around the room, flour flying from her fingers. "It turned out to be Landon's house."

"Wow, so you ended up dating the boss, huh?"

She grins at me. "I couldn't stand him at first. He was so full of himself and bossy, but he grew on me."

"Dare said he's not conceited, he's confident." I roll my eyes.

Zoe laughs and takes the cutting board full of chopped vegetables from me, dumping them into the dressing. "Confidence isn't an issue for any of them. They're all sweethearts under that cocky exterior, though. How long have you been seeing each other?"

I'm not sure what to say. "Oh, we're not...really dating or anything. He only invited me because I didn't have plans. We're just neighbors."

Zoe cocks an eyebrow. "Uh-huh."

"It's true," I laugh.

Zoe looks up from stirring a pot of boiling potatoes and points the spoon at me. "I haven't known Dare for too long, but Landon grew up with him, and this is the first time he's ever introduced a woman to his friends."

That makes me pause. "Really?"

"Really." She peeks at me. "And don't even try to tell me you aren't interested. There isn't a single woman alive who wouldn't climb all over that man."

We laugh, and she pours me another glass of wine. With all the food either prepared or finishing up in the oven, she takes a break and sits across from me. It feels good to laugh and share in some girl talk. Dare was right, I like Zoe.

"Let's go bug the guys. We don't want them getting too comfortable without us," she says, and we head to the living room.

Dare and Justus sit on either end of the couch while Jeremy and Landon occupy two oversize recliners. Zoe walks over to Landon, and he instantly pulls her into his lap, dropping a kiss on her lips. Dare grins up at me and grabs my wrist, tugging me to sit beside him. His arm slides around me like it's the most natural thing in the world, and Zoe gives me an I-told-you-so smile.

"Having fun?" he asks in a low voice.

I don't get a chance to answer before I feel a warm body on my other side. Like right by my side. Justus grins at me, a mischievous glint in his eye. His thigh is flush with mine when he says, "So, Ayda. How do you feel about male entertainers?"

What the hell does he mean, entertainers? Justus is obviously trying to rile Dare up, and by the look on Dare's face, it's working. Snuggling against Dare's side, I reply, "If you're trying to tell me you're a hooker, I'm not interested."

Everyone laughs and Dare shoves Justus off the couch with one hand. "I'm not a hooker, although if I wanted to charge, plenty of women would pay for my services," Justus announces, returning to the couch, this time staying on his side.

"He's a stripper," Zoe informs me.

"Exotic dancer!" Justus insists.

The rest of the evening flies by. Dinner is delicious, and everyone is gathered in the living room when Landon suddenly appears from a back room dressed in a three piece suit and drops to one knee in front of Zoe.

The room falls quiet while he professes his love and asks her to marry him. Pure joy shines in her eyes as she accepts, and he slides the ring on her finger. Everyone hugs her, and the guys slap Landon on the back, congratulating him.

Watching them all, it hits me how much I've been missing out on. The guys torment and tease each other, but there's a wealth of love in this room. The easy way they talk and relate to each other, I haven't had that with anyone but Sadie since I was a teenager. There are some things I've accepted I can't have. My scarred body ruins any chance of a sex life, which kills the possibility of love and marriage, but maybe I can have more than I do now. More friends, closer ties, real relationships that aren't romantic. I feel something I haven't felt for a long time. Hope.

It's dark out when Dare and I say our goodbyes and start for home. With all the leftovers Zoe insisted I take, I won't have to cook for a week. When I unlock my apartment door, Dare follows me in like he lives here, kicking off his shoes and getting comfortable on my couch.

After putting the leftovers in the fridge, I sit in the chair across from him. "Thanks for inviting me tonight. I had fun. Your friends are great."

His gaze rolls over me. "You're welcome. Now, get your cute little ass over here."

"It's late. I should probably go to bed," I mumble.

He scoffs and scoops me out of my seat, putting me on his lap.

How am I going to get out of this? I know he wants to fuck me, and damn do I want to let him, but he won't feel the same after he sees me naked. The last guy could overlook the facial scars too, but one glance at the rest of me, and he was done. All I can see is the look of disgust on his face as he fucked me while trying not to look or touch the affected areas. I don't want to see that expression on Dare's face.

Dare is one persistent man, and I know he won't give up. Worse, I know I can't resist him. Maybe it's better to lay the truth out on the table right now and get it over with. I get to my feet before he can stop me and pace the room. "You don't want to fuck me, Dare."

"Babe, I've never wanted anything more, and I know you feel the same way. Now tell me what's got you so twisted up."

A million excuses run through my mind.

We're too different.

I'm gay.

You sleep around too much.

He'll never believe I'm a lesbian, and as for him sleeping around, it occurs to me I haven't heard one woman in his apartment since we started talking.

I settle for the truth. "The scars on my face are only a fraction of the damage. The right side of my body is covered. It isn't pretty, and tends to make men run for the hills. Trust me, it's an instant turn off."

Anger ignites in his eyes. He stalks over to me, grabs my shoulders and stares into my eyes. "Anyone who ran from you because of a few scars isn't a man. He's a dick."

"It's ugly," I murmur.

Ignoring me, he continues, "There isn't a damn thing about you that's ugly." He leans in and presses his hard body to mine. His voice is soft and raspy in my ear. "You have no idea how many times I've watched you by the pool, laid out in that bikini."

My jaw drops. I was always careful to sunbathe at off hours, when most people are at work. The tan helps cover some of the scars. I didn't think he'd seen me.

He takes advantage of my speechless shock, and presses his lips to mine. Damn, the man can kiss. He makes me feel like I've never been kissed before. The way he takes my mouth with such passion and force, like he can't help himself, wipes away the memories of long ago kisses that could never measure up. All the self-conscious thoughts that run through my head during moments like this are absent, lost in the sensation of his tongue stroking mine, his hands undressing me as we make our way down the hall.

Suddenly, I'm staring at my bedroom ceiling. "The light," I mumble, watching him strip.

"Stays on." He's back in bossy mode. Before I can protest, I'm yanked to the end of the bed, and his face is between my legs.

A low chuckle is followed by a wicked smile when I gasp and instinctively twist away. His arms lock around my legs, holding them open and leaving me vulnerable to his talented mouth. Just the sight of his dark head between my legs, his large hands on my thighs, is almost enough to make me come. I've never been with someone so ruggedly handsome, so strong... so *male*.

I'm close, right on the edge when he stops, drawing a frustrated cry from my throat.

"Not yet, baby. Not until I'm inside you." He delivers little kisses up my stomach and plants his hot mouth over my nipple, drawing it in, licking and sucking, before moving to show the other the same attention until I'm half out of my mind.

It's not until he pauses to roll on a condom that my brain clears enough to notice what's coming at me. I don't know whether to weep with joy or run away screaming at the size of him.

"It's been a while," I confess, licking my lips.

"I'll go easy…this time," he says, trapping my body under his. Never has a threat sounded so promising. He's careful not to put his full weight on me—he'd squash me like a bug—and I wrap my legs around him.

His face is a mask of concentration while he works his way into me with short, slow strokes. He's barely halfway in, and I feel like he could split me in half, but it doesn't stop me from wanting more. I spread my legs wider, and he slides in another inch.

"That's it, you can take me." His next thrust is harder, more determined, and my nails dig into his firm ass when he buries himself completely. Intense eyes lock with mine. "Are you okay?"

Nodding frantically, I squeeze his ass, trying to get him to move again. "Please."

"Please what, Ayda?" He's not teasing me. There's not an ounce of humor in his voice.

"Fuck me." I move my hips beneath him, trying to take what I want, and his wicked smile returns.

He pulls out slowly, then eases back in, making me

moan as the pain turns to mind numbing pleasure. "Fuck, I knew you'd feel good," he groans, increasing his pace. The sensations bombarding me make me want to close my eyes, but I don't want to miss a second of the display of sweaty flexing muscles above me.

His finger slips down to rub my clit, and I lose all control, crying out as I'm struck by the strongest orgasm of my life. He never slows, dragging out the pleasure until I feel like I could die of it.

He pulls out of me, rolls me onto my side, and pulls my leg back over his, entering me from behind in one swift thrust. "Oh god!"

His mouth is on my nape, sucking on the sensitive skin. Tingles cascade down my body while his hot breath fills my ear. "You like that?"

I push back against him, urging him on, and he catches both of my hands in his, pinning them to my stomach. I'm completely restrained and at his mercy when he starts pounding into me. The man is going to fuck me half to death, but I'm sure as hell not complaining. Another orgasm rolls through me in slow, pulsing waves, and my name leaves his lips in a low growl as he finishes deep inside me.

We lie still, catching our breath for a few moments before he gets up to dispose of the condom. A few seconds later, he's back in my bed, pulling me into his arms.

Isn't it supposed to be the guy who falls asleep right after sex? I can hardly hold my eyes open. My last thought before I succumb to the warmth and comfort of his body wrapped around mine is that I never once worried about him seeing or touching my scars.

———

I wake with Dare still holding me, his large palm cupping one of my breasts. He grins down at me when I peek up at him. "If you're a boob man, you're out of luck," I tease.

"The hell I am." He tweaks my nipple. "They're perfect. But if you must know, I'm a leg man, and your legs are gorgeous."

I'm facing him with my head on his chest, and he pulls my leg over his hip, caressing it. Years of dancing have given me lean, solid thighs and sculpted calves. It's one part of my body I'm not self-conscious about. His hand wanders up over my stomach and across the scars on my ribs, making me tense up. I was too distracted by what he was making me feel last night to worry about it, but now I'm lying naked in a pool of sunlight, exposing every marred inch.

"Relax, baby." Rolling onto his side, and propping his head on his hand, he continues to caress and stroke my skin, his fingers trailing lightly over the scars on my arm and shoulder. Sympathetic eyes meet mine, and I have to swallow the lump in my throat. No one has ever touched me like this, with reverence instead of disgust or morbid curiosity.

"Will you tell me what happened?" he asks softly.

Against my better judgement, I find myself explaining. "They're chemical burns. When I was eighteen, I got a dancing scholarship that one of the other students wanted. She and her boyfriend planned to sabotage me. Being ranked second to me, she knew she was the next in line for the scholarship if I dropped out. Her boyfriend waited for me after class. I was always the last one to leave the studio and I usually parked in the alley out back. I didn't see it coming, didn't even know who threw it on me until later when the police saw the video. There was a security camera that picked up the whole thing."

He tries to keep his voice soft, but I can hear the anger in it when he asks, "Is the asshole still locked up?"

Sitting up, I grab my shirt and pull it on. "He never went to jail. He's a senator's son. He got probation."

"You're fucking kidding me." His expression is fierce. "What about the girl?"

"She got the scholarship and dances for a company in Chicago last I heard." I try not to sound bitter, but it's hard. After all they took from me, they got what they wanted, their happy ending, while I'll spend the rest of my life scarred and probably alone.

"What's his name?" Dare demands.

"What?" The bed creaks when I get up and slide on a pair of panties.

"The senator's son. What's his name?" He's sitting up in my bed, the sheet at his waist, looking like he could tear someone in two.

"It doesn't matter," I sigh. "I don't want to talk about it anymore, okay?"

He gets to his feet and stalks over to me, stark naked. "Tell me who he is, Ayda. I'll fucking kill him."

I believe him, too. Maybe I should be scared of the barely restrained violence I see in his eyes, but he's pissed on my behalf, because someone hurt me. Approaching him slowly, I press my forehead to his wide chest. "I don't want to talk about him."

With a sigh, I feel him relax a little. His hand cups the

back of my head, stroking my hair. He slides a finger under my chin, tilting my head until I'm looking him in those blue eyes. "I'll never let anyone hurt you. I protect what's mine."

"I'm yours?" I whisper.

"Mine," he replies, placing a firm kiss on my lips. The ring of his phone breaks the moment.

"Answer your phone." I grin at him while he pulls on his jeans. "I'm going to grab that pie out of the fridge for breakfast."

Smiling, he smacks my ass before picking up his phone.

He's sitting in my bed wearing only his jeans, leaning back against the wall when I return with the apple pie and two forks. It's exactly how I pictured him on his own bed all those nights while we talked through the wall.

I sit cross legged beside him and we dig into the pie, laughing and talking until he gets a text message that makes him frown. After he replies to it, he sighs and reaches for his shirt. "I have to go."

"Is everything okay?"

"Everything's fine. I owe a friend of mine a favor, and he needs me to work for him the next few days."

"On Thanksgiving weekend? That sucks." I open my dresser to get some clean clothes. "Maybe we could meet for dinner tomorrow night?"

"The job is in Ohio. I should be back by Monday afternoon." He gives me a heart stopping smile. "I'll call you, okay?"

"Sure." A quick kiss lands on my lips, then he's out the door. I'm full of questions, but I don't want to be too

demanding or clingy. He doesn't owe me any expla-
nations.

Despite that, I spend the next few minutes in the
shower dwelling on what just happened. What kind of
work is he doing for his friend? He works in internet
security, so I assume it's related, but why would that take
him to Ohio over a holiday weekend?

My typical self-doubt creeps in. Maybe it was a way
out. An excuse to get away now that he got what he
wanted. He certainly wouldn't be the first not to want it
again. Then I remember the way he looked at me. The
way he touched me, without an ounce of disgust or pity,
only heat and lust in his eyes.

I'm doing what I always do, overthinking and
assuming the worst. He had to work, and I'll see him in a
few days. It's no big deal.

Sadie shows up at my door as soon as I'm dressed.
"Hey, you're back early. How did it go?" I ask. Sadie
wasn't looking forward to spending Thanksgiving at her
father's house, especially since he just got remarried.

"It was tense and uncomfortable, as usual." She flops
onto my couch. "Now tell me all about your date with
sexy tats."

"It wasn't a date," I insist.

"Fine, whatever, how did it go?"

"We had a good time. His friends are nice."

Sadie gives me an exasperated look. "And?"

"And he fucked my brains out."

Her eyes bug out. "I knew it! Okay, tell me about it
and don't skimp on the details. A guy that big, I'll bet
he's hung like a horse, isn't he?"

Sitting beside her, I hold my hands out in front of me,

showing her how long he was. "Damn near split me in two."

"When are you going to see him again?"

"He's out of town for a few days for work. Probably Monday."

She flings her arms around me. "I'm so happy for you!"

"Okay, woman, calm down. It was one night," I laugh.

"You don't invite a woman to meet your friends if all you want is a one night stand. Did he ask to see you again?"

"Not exactly, but he said he'd call and..." I hesitate before adding. "He said I'm his."

Her eyebrows jump. "You're his?"

"He said, 'You're mine and I protect what's mine.'"

Sadie's eyes roll back, and she groans. "It's not enough he's a damn mountain of inked up muscle, he's an alpha male too. If you screw this up, I will kill you."

"Alpha male?" I scoff. "You read too many romance books."

"Ayda, the man fucked your brains out, then claimed you and swore to protect you. He's an alpha. Christ, tell me he has a brother or something," she pleads.

"He has some hot friends. You'd love his friend Justus. Lean and muscled with blond curls. He works at a strip club."

"I'm going to need the name of that club."

Sadie hangs out for a few hours before heading off to visit a patient.

The rest of my day is spent catching up on work. After only getting a few hours of sleep the night before,

I'm exhausted. I fall into bed, making sure my phone is on charge beside me in case Dare calls.

It's not the phone that wakes me, though. The steady banging on the other side of the bedroom wall invades my dreams and it takes me a few seconds to realize it's real.

What the hell? Dare isn't supposed to be back for a few days. What is he doing over there?

A long moan followed by a high pitched giggle answers my question. You got to be fucking kidding me.

I sink back into my pillows and desperately try to think of any other explanation for what I'm hearing. It's no use. I know sex sounds when I hear them. The bed slams against the wall and whatever skank he's brought home cries out with every bang.

He isn't really audible, only an occasional grunt or moan. There's still a chance it's not him. He said he'd be out of town. Maybe he has a roommate? I know it's unlikely. He's never mentioned a roommate, and the next thing I hear destroys any hope.

"Yes! God, yes, Dare! Don't stop!"

Disappointment floods through me. I should have known all that "you're mine" talk was bullshit. And being called out of town for work. I can't lie here and listen to them any longer. Instead, I grab my blanket and move to the couch.

Like there's any chance in hell I can sleep now. Staring at the ceiling, I blink back the tears trying to form. It's not like I'm in love with the guy. I shouldn't be this upset, but I am. Against my better judgement, I trusted him and told him what happened to me. That's something only my closest friend knew. His reaction to seeing me naked was so reassuring that I dropped my guard and actually let myself believe he was attracted to me, scars and all.

Was it the scars that scared him away, or is he just another asshole who fucks as many women as possible? What hurts the most is that he knows I can hear him. That I know he didn't go out of town and only used that as a way to escape. He's showing me exactly how little last night meant by making me listen to him fuck another woman while I'm still sore from him.

Fuck it. Lesson learned. I won't fall for any of his bullshit again, although I doubt that'll be an issue since I never plan to speak to him again.

Sunlight beams in through the living room curtains, and I give up trying to sleep, deciding instead to focus on work. Thankfully, Lisa calls a few hours later to ask if I can meet with Ryan to work on his routine, and I jump at the opportunity. Sitting in my apartment and picturing Dare wrapped around some woman next door is torture.

When I check my phone, I see a missed call and a voicemail from him. *"Hey, beautiful. Just wanted you to know I'm thinking of you. Talk to you later."*

Is he serious? I guess he thinks I'm desperate enough to take what I can get, but does he honestly expect me to be okay with being lied to? That he can tell me he's going out of town and I'll just pretend I didn't hear him banging someone else?

I knew there was a reason I gave up on men. Sighing, I delete the message. Asshole or not, I'll miss him.

Ryan is waiting at the dance studio when I arrive, and we get right to work. I throw myself into the choreography, dancing alongside him until we get it perfect. There are a few moves that I change, things he can do that my limited range-of-motion won't allow. When the music ends again, we drop to the floor to catch our breath. The sound of applause erupts from behind us. A group of dancers and parents from the advanced class were watching. We used the main studio this time, and I didn't even notice them come in.

"That was amazing!" a woman says, approaching me. "Are you available to do private lessons? My daughter is having trouble with a new routine."

"I'm sorry. I'm helping Ryan as a favor to Lisa. I don't normally teach."

Disappointed, the woman nods. "Well, if you change your mind, Lisa has my information. I'd love to have you work with my daughter."

After assuring the lady I'd call if I became available, I say goodbye to Ryan and change into my street clothes.

Lisa catches me before I can leave. "Ayda! Ryan's routine looks amazing. I've had requests from three different parents for private lessons."

There's no denying the little spike of happiness I feel. I've avoided dancing in public ever since I was attacked. To me, dance is about displaying the human body with grace and beauty, and my beauty is long gone. I assumed it would be awkward, if not downright horrifying to have to face those in the dance world with such a scarred body. It's been suggested before that I teach, but I didn't want to deal with cringing parents and kids who may be repulsed or even frightened.

Maybe I was wrong. Working with Ryan has brought back the joy I used to feel when I danced. Maybe I can still be a part of the world I love, instead of dancing at night to block out the loneliness. I could pass on what I know and help these kids accomplish what I couldn't.

Lisa watches my internal struggle. "I'm not asking you to teach full time," she points out, her voice soft. "Just a few hours a week, one-on-one with the students who are competing."

"Okay," I blurt.

Lisa's eyebrows jump, and a smile bursts across her face. "You'll do it?"

"Let's say, two days per week? Two students per day? And you choose the students."

"Yes! Great! Fantastic! I'll set it up!"

Walking to my car, I worry over my impulsive decision, but I also realize something. I'm looking forward to it.

My mood plummets when my phone rings, and Dare's number pops up. I quickly reject the call. The man has balls the size of Texas. He has to know I heard him fucking someone else not even twenty-four hours after he left my bed. It's not like we're exclusive, but I'm also not getting involved with a guy who fucks anything that moves.

I knew sleeping with him would be a mistake, that I'd lose him as a friend, when I don't have a lot of those to sacrifice. Maybe we'll eventually be able to go back to hanging out, but I won't be fucking him again.

Admittedly, he's been good for me. He's given me some of my confidence back, and I'm not going to go back to hiding in my apartment just because it didn't work out. Maybe there are some things I can't have out of life, like love or marriage, but that doesn't mean I can't try for more than I have now. Like friendship and a fulfilling career.

Don't get me wrong, I like the work I do in graphic art, and I'll balance it with teaching, but I need something to do that'll force me to leave the house. Sadie will be thrilled when I tell her.

CHAPTER
EIGHT

DARE

When Mason called, I assumed he needed me to hack something or find out some information on someone. I didn't expect a security job, but I couldn't say no. He and his brothers who run Striking Back, a domestic violence shelter, always step in whenever we need them, and they must be short handed to ask me to guard a family when I've never done it before.

He calls me when I'm almost to the house. "All you have to do is stay with them. I've moved them over one hundred fifty miles from her husband. It's highly unlikely that he'll find them, but I need someone there just in case. Since you're big as a damn house, you're nominated. Alex will be there Monday morning to relieve you.".

"Got it." Three days trapped in a house with strangers. I'm glad I brought my laptop.

Ayda has given me next to no information about who hurt her, but since she revealed it was a senator's son and how long ago it happened, I know I can find out. The senator in question may have been able to keep it off the news, but the internet is not as forgiving. There will be blog posts and chats about it. I just have to dig them up.

My mind wanders back to Ayda. Her hot little body under me, panting and calling my name. I knew there was a dirty girl hiding beneath that reserved manner. She can't hide from me. I could see the fear and trepidation in her expression when I ran my fingers over her scars, and it pissed me off. What the hell has she heard from those past assholes to make her ashamed of something that was done to her, not by her?

The thin, raised skin does nothing to detract from her beauty, and I hate that she can't see how attractive she really is. I've only been away from her for a few hours and I already can't wait to get my hands on her again.

I'm not going to try to resist her anymore. There's a lot she doesn't know about me, and after she trusted me enough to tell me what happened to her, I have to come clean about my past. Even if she doesn't hold that against me, there's the fact I still break the law. Will it matter to her that it's for a good reason, or will she run when she finds out?

Landon and the guys would never stop breaking my balls if they knew how twisted up this little scrap of a woman has me.

I'm met by Devon, one of Mason's security men, when I pull into the drive. He fills me in on the family I'll be protecting. "Sharon and the kids are inside. There isn't much for you to do. Keep an eye on things and don't let anyone inside the house. The local authorities know what's going on. If you have any problems, don't hesitate to call them. Sharon knows the code for the house alarm."

"How dangerous is this guy?"

Devon shakes his head. "He's a minimal threat, if any. Just about pissed himself when Parker and I came to move them out of their apartment. But she's scared, and we want to make sure she doesn't give in and go back to him, so the farther away we could get her, the better."

He accompanies me inside and introduces me to Sharon and her six year old twins before leaving. Sharon gives me a slight smile, then returns to playing with Legos with her boys. It's clear she'd rather I not bother her, so I head back to the guest bedroom to drop off my bag, then take a seat on the front porch and pull out my laptop. I want to call Ayda, but it's only been a few hours. This woman is turning me into a little bitch.

The next few hours are spent searching for Ayda's attacker. Whoever this guy is, his father has done a good job of burying the story, but not good enough. I help myself to some sealed court papers, and within minutes I have his name in front of me.

Talbot Coulter, age twenty-seven. This guy is a Grade-A asshole with a record going back to his eighteenth birthday. There's a sealed juvenile record as well, but I don't even bother with it. I've seen all I need to see.

His father, Senator Montgomery Coulter, has been bailing him out of trouble for years, and by the looks of it he has more than one judge in his pocket. Add another name to my revenge list. Ayda isn't the only woman he's hurt over the years. The same judge dismissed a case brought against him by a young woman at his college for sexual assault a year after Ayda's attack.

A search using Talbot's name and Ayda's steers me to an article that names the dancer who put him up to it. It isn't hard to find information on her once I have her name, since she doesn't even have her Facebook profile set to private. It gets easier and easier to find people since the world is now steeped in narcissism. Everyone posts everything about their lives as if no one is watching.

I'm not sure what I want to do about her yet. I won't use violence against a woman, even one as deserving as her, but there are lots of other ways to screw with someone's life. They scarred Ayda for life, and not only physically. They *are* going to pay.

Sharon is getting the kids to bed when I go back inside. She watches me check the locks on the doors and windows before arming the alarm. Approaching me hesitantly, she asks, "Do you think we could take the boys down the street to the park tomorrow? Devon went with us before. They're getting a little restless being cooped up."

If Devon took them, it must be okay. From what he and Mason have told me, he's keeping a guard here as a precaution and to make Sharon feel secure. "Sure, let me know when you'd like to go."

"Thank you." She gives me a quick smile and retires to her bedroom.

The last couple of nights with little sleep are starting to catch up with me. It's a good night to crash early. Something tells me those boys will be up with the sun.

The sound of giggling wakes me and it takes me a second to remember where I am. Dragging myself out of bed, I do a quick check of the house and yard. Everything's fine. I take a quick shower and grab a cup of coffee before accompanying Sharon and her boys to the park. It's only two blocks away, but I check with Mason because I'm not sure what his protocol would be for leaving the house. When he texts to let me know they have Sharon's ex under surveillance and he's not even in the state, I take a seat on the park bench to relax.

It hasn't even been twenty-four hours since I left Ayda's, but I want to hear her voice. Instead of getting an answer, her voicemail message plays. She's probably still asleep.

The day drags by. Sharon and her kids don't need anything from me but to be present. I spend most of my time researching the Coulters, the judge, and the dancer who's responsible for Ayda's pain.

When everyone is in bed for the night, I check my phone one last time and see Ayda still hasn't called. When I call her phone, it only rings twice, then goes to voicemail, which means she rejected the call and *sent* me to voicemail. What the hell?

The next two days seem to last a week. Ayda continues to ignore my calls and texts. All I want to do is get home to see what the hell went wrong since I left her apartment Friday morning. I'm in my car and on the highway minutes after Alex shows to relieve me.

Ayda's car isn't in the parking lot when I return, and like a whipped bitch, I spend most of the day peeking out the window, watching for her to get back. I'm in a pissed off mood by that night when Landon shows up.

"Hey, asshole. I thought you were coming to work today. Did the job for Mason last longer than you expected?" he asks, helping himself to a beer from my fridge.

"Guess I forgot," I grumble, flipping through a hundred channels of shit on the TV.

"Uh-huh." He stares at me, trying not to grin. "And would this new winning attitude have anything to do with the chick you brought to Thanksgiving dinner?"

"Nope, just a reaction to the sight of your ugly face. Where's your fiancée? She get sick of you already?"

"I wore her out, put her out of commission for the night." Landon sits back and props his foot on his knee. "So, did you fuck her yet?"

"Are you trying to get your ass kicked? Because there are easier ways."

Landon laughs. "This woman has really gotten to you, hasn't she?"

"We fucked and now she won't talk to me."

"What did you do?"

"Hell if I know. Everything was fine when I left, but she won't return my calls or texts."

He suppresses a grin. "And you haven't just bullied your way into her apartment to confront her?"

"She hasn't been home."

"Well, she lives next door. She can't ignore you forever."

"What's going on with the new forum? Was Justus able to infiltrate?" I ask, changing the subject.

"He's in, but I'm not sure it's a good thing. He's hyped up about this one for some reason. You know how he gets. It's a big ring of human traffickers, encompassing three states, so we can't screw this one up or go all vigilante. We need to cover our bases and make sure we can safely report it to the police. We're having trouble nailing down all the addresses, which is why I'm here. Justus could use some help."

I can't spend all my time stalking the parking lot for Ayda when I should be working. "Give me a minute to get my shit together and I'll follow you over."

Justus and Jeremy are sitting at their computers, typing away when I arrive. Landon walks in ahead of me and announces, "I found him mooning over the girl next door."

They all break into laughter. "Don't make me stuff you into a tanning bed," I growl.

"Prison has made you very unpleasant," Landon retorts.

That's when you know you're close friends, when you can use a horrific disease or terrible prison stint to insult each other and laugh over it.

Dragging a chair over to sit beside Justus, I stare at the screen. "Fill me in on what I missed."

We spend half the night working. Justus chats with the traffickers, pretending to be an interested customer who's shopping for the perfect girl while I try to nail down the IP addresses. These guys are pros, and know how to conceal themselves well. A little after three a.m. the screen goes blank.

"What the fuck?" Justus shouts, slamming his fists on the desk.

"What happened?" Jeremy asks, approaching us.

"They shut it down! Fuck! I was so close!" Justus paces the room, clutching the back of his head.

It's disappointing because we know they haven't shut

down the operation, only moved it to a new location. They suspect something's up. I don't know if it's us they suspect or if something else alarmed them. If they aren't suspicious of Justus, they'll get in touch, since they won't want to let a serious buyer go, but if we triggered the move, we may never find them again. Sadly, it's not the first time it's happened.

"Are you still connected on the gaming profile?" Jeremy asks, and Justus rushes back to his computer.

"So far." It's another way traffickers can communicate, using chat and messaging from large MMORPG games. They aren't generally watched the way other avenues are.

"Give it a day and see what happens," Landon suggests, trying to calm Justus.

"In the meantime, I need your help with something," I tell him. He listens while I explain what happened to Ayda and what I intend to do about it.

Justus's grin would chill the blood of an average man, but I'm happy to see it. "We're going to fuck them up," he promises.

It's nearly four in the morning when I get home and fall into bed. Ayda's car is in the parking lot, but her apartment is quiet. I'm dying to bust in and demand to know what her problem is, but I'm not going to wake her. She'll think I'm a psycho. I'm sure I'll catch her tomorrow.

The ringing of my phone wakes me up, and my sister's perky voice greets me when I answer. "Derek! Hi, I got your message. Sorry, it took me a while to call back. I've been busy."

"College kicking your ass?" I tease.

"As usual. I found a great study group, though. And I met a guy."

She sounds happy, and it puts a smile on my face. "What's the dude's name and how far do I have to drive to kick his ass?"

She giggles. "His name is Jake, and you aren't kicking anything. He's a real sweet guy. You'll like him."

"Are you bringing him home for Christmas?"

There's a pause before she replies, "That's kind of what I'm calling about. I'm not coming back for Christmas. There's a big party here I want to go to."

I can't blame her. She's young and full of life. There's nothing here for her anymore. "Be careful and don't drink anything that's been out of your sight," I warn.

"I'm always careful. I promise I'll come and visit soon, okay?"

"You'd better. Don't make me come up there."

"I have to go. Love you."

"Love you." I barely have the words out and she's already hung up. A smile stretches across my face. She's having fun, living her life and enjoying herself. It's everything I wanted for her, and hearing how happy she is makes my time behind bars worth it.

On my way to the shower, I stop to look out the window to see if Ayda's car is parked outside. She's gone again. For a woman who works at home, she sure is gone a lot lately. Is she trying to avoid me, or is it a coincidence?

It's late afternoon when I meet the guys back at ISH, and I find everyone in a better mood than last night. Someone messaged Justus through the gaming site with the link of the new forum, so apparently we weren't the threat they were worried about. He has also gathered some information for me.

"This guy is a real dickhole," he says. "And he gets it honestly. His father is just as bad. I called in a favor and managed to get the senator's private email, and I was able to get into his personal computer. It's full of porn—most of it's gay porn—and some may be underage. He has some amateur stuff featuring him and two boys who look a little young for eighteen. Even if they are legal, this guy is a republican who campaigns with an anti-gay platform."

"You're thinking the best thing to do is go public? Splash it all over the tabloids?" We've never gone that direction before.

"It's a start."

"It's more than a start. Talbot has been charged four times in the past ten years. Twice for sexual assault and twice for aggravated assault. All four times, Judge Dalton has been assigned the case. All four times, the charges have been dismissed for lack of evidence. I cross referenced the senator's bank records and Talbot's with the judge's. A few days before each charge was dismissed, a hundred grand was transferred into the judge's account. The first three were sent from the senator's account, the last one from Talbot's. There's no doubt they've been paying him off."

"They weren't very smart about it," Justus snorts. "Give me a few days to try to track the porn. If the boys are underage, we may want to handle it differently."

Of course, we don't want to publicize a video of underage kids. If that turns out to be the case, that much of what we've found will be turned over to authorities.

"I won't do anything for now, but I don't want to wait long. This asshole has gotten away with too much for too long. We can try them in the court of public opinion first, but I want the father and son behind bars. If we can't manage that, I can't promise I won't feed Talbot to the pigs."

Justus grins and slaps me on the back. "I get it, man."

It's the middle of the night when I get home again, and Ayda's apartment is quiet. One way or another, I'm getting in touch with her tomorrow. These days apart have done nothing to make me forget her. Just the opposite, I want her now more than ever.

As soon as my eyes pop open the next morning, I hear Ayda's shower running. Finally. I'm going over there and she's going to explain why the hell she's been ignoring me. I'm dressed and at her door a few minutes after the sound of her shower stops.

My knock on her door goes unanswered, but I can sense her standing on the other side. I swear, I'm doomed to have all our conversations through a damn wall.

"Ayda, I know you're there. Just open up and talk to me."

After a few seconds of silence, I add, "I'm not going away. I'll wait right here until you come out."

The door is jerked open, and her glare nearly cuts me in half. "What do you want?"

She stands there in a pair of form fitting jeans and a clingy sweater. I want to throw her over my shoulder, march her back to the bedroom and remind her why we're good together. The look on her face screams *don't touch me,* so I settle for stepping inside the door where she can't lock me out before I figure out what pissed her off.

"Why have you been ignoring my calls?"

She crosses her arms and takes a step back. "I've been busy."

"Bullshit. You're pissed. Tell me why."

Her ears turn pink, and she presses her lips together so hard they nearly disappear. "Un-fucking-believable," she hisses.

"I thought we had a good time Friday night. What's changed since then?"

"Friday night was a mistake. It never should've happened and it sure as hell won't happen again."

My fingers wrap around her wrist when she starts to walk away. "It wasn't a fucking mistake." I'm struggling to control my anger.

She takes a deep breath. "Yes, it was, because I'm not one of these needy bitches who's going to follow you around and lick your balls, hoping you'll choose me. I have no desire to try to compete with whatever trash you dragged home Friday night."

Silence fills the room while I stand there, stunned. "I was in Ohio Friday night."

Her stare is incredulous. "Do you think I'm fucking stupid? I heard you! You *know* I can hear you! And I got the message just fine when she was screaming your name. I'm done. Now, get out!" She raises her voice and shoves at me, which would be kind of cute if I weren't so pissed. She can't weigh one twenty soaking wet and her head only comes to my chest.

I notice another neighbor watching, a young woman with her little boy. The wary expression on her face says she's ready to intervene. Shit. I don't need cops showing up over an argument.

When Ayda shoves me again, I take a step back onto the landing. "We're not done, Ayda," I warn, before she slams the door.

What the hell just happened? Confused and pissed off, I stalk back to my apartment, my mind running in overdrive. I've dealt with some of the worst human beings alive when I was locked up, men bigger and more brutal than me, but this little scrap of a woman has me pulling my hair out.

There's no way she heard fucking coming from... damn it. Justus. Justus has a key to my apartment and he knew I'd be gone. I'll kill him. Grabbing my phone from the table, I nearly crack the screen hitting his name in my contacts.

"Dare, what's up?" he answers.

"Did you bang some chick in my apartment Friday night?" I demand.

He laughs. He fucking *laughs*, and I'm glad he isn't in front of me right now. "I changed your sheets, man. I didn't think you'd mind. I worked a bachelorette party and the chick was all over me. I didn't want her to know where I lived."

"And you gave her my name," I bark.

He pauses. "How did you know that? Oh hell, did she show back up?"

"Because Ayda heard her screaming it, you fuck-wad! That's why she won't have anything to do with me."

"Oh fuck. I'm sorry. I didn't realize. I'll tell Ayda. If you'll give me her number—"

"I'm not giving you her number! You're going to get your ass over here and explain it to her face!"

"All right! Yeah, give me a few minutes. I'm on my way." I end the call, toss the phone on the couch, and open my door just in time to see Ayda's car speed off. Damn it.

"Leave her alone. She doesn't need your shit," a voice warns. A young woman is walking away from Ayda's front door, her blond hair blowing around her face. I've seen her at Ayda's before, so she must be a friend.

"I need to talk to her. Where is she going?"

The woman scoffs. "Away from you as fast as she can." She shakes her head. "She finally puts herself out there, and you turn out to be another asshole."

"I'm not...look, it was a misunderstanding. She heard a friend of mine using my apartment. I didn't know about it and I'm going to kick his ass, but he's on his way now to tell her the truth."

Her hand perches on her hip while she thinks about it. "It wasn't you? She heard the woman say your name."

Sighing, I run a hand through my hair. "He used my name to get laid. Look, it's a long story, but I need to find her."

Blue eyes glare at me. "She's been through hell. If you're just trying to get laid, you need to move on to someone else."

"I'm not. I..." I rub my palm across my face. "I care about her, okay? I need her to know it wasn't me. She's hurt."

The woman finally smiles. "She'll be at the On Pointe Dance Academy from five until nine. Wait until class is over. If you cause a scene and embarrass her, she'll hate you."

"Thank you," I sigh, already counting down the hours until nine o'clock.

"Be good to her, or I'll tear your nuts off and throw them in White River."

CHAPTER
NINE

AYDA

"He did what?" Sadie demands. The water is out in her neighborhood, so she came to my apartment to shower.

"Lied and said he was going out of town, then fucked some other woman the night after me, where he knew I could hear it. I assume it was his way of letting me know our night didn't mean anything. Not that I thought it did, but still." I flop onto the couch.

"It was dick move," she finishes.

"I'm done with him. It sucks because I really liked him, you know?" One peek up at my friend brings a smile to my face. She's as pissed as I am.

"You can do so much better, girl."

A snort comes out when I laugh. "Have you seen him?"

She joins me with a chuckle. "Yeah, why do the hottest ones always have to be assholes?"

"Better to know now, I guess, before I got in too deep."

Sadie hugs me. "I'm sorry. Don't let this keep you from trying again. You've been much more outgoing since you met him."

"I agreed to give private lessons at your sister's school," I tell her, and her face lights up.

"Really? That's awesome! I'm so proud of you."

We're interrupted by a knock at the door. Sadie looks through the peephole and whispers, "It's him. Want me to tear him a new one?"

Tempting, but I need to fight my own battles. When he refuses to leave and threatens to wait me out, my anger boils over. I'm not taking any more shit from him. "Wait in the bedroom," I tell Sadie. "I can handle this."

She steps out of view, and he barges through the door when I open it. I leave it open, making it clear he isn't coming past my foyer. The conversation that ensues is unbelievable. I expect him to apologize, claim he was drunk or something, but instead he says it wasn't him. Seriously? That's the best he has? *I know you heard fucking, and the girl screamed my name, but it wasn't me.* It's such an insult to my intelligence that I lose my temper, scream at him, and shove him out the door.

His last words ring in my head as Sadie rejoins me in the living room. "We're not done, Ayda."

I wish that were true, that things didn't have to be this way, but I'm not sharing him with other women. "I've got to get to the dance school. Just lock up when you leave," I tell Sadie, and escape to the solitude of my car.

The undercurrent of sadness and disappointment I

feel is tempered with anger which helps propel me through the next few hours. Ryan performs the routine beautifully, and I'm confident he's ready for the upcoming competition. The new student I'm working with isn't enrolled in this competition. We have plenty of time to get her ready for the next one that's over a month away.

We choose her music and begin to work out her strengths and weaknesses. We need to know what to work on and what to include in the routine. Her mother comes to pick her up a little early, and thanks me profusely for working with her. I smile, nod, and say all the right words, but my mind is still stuck on Dare.

The school is empty since it's now after hours, and I decide to spend a few minutes dancing alone. The stereo blares, and the music takes me far away from all my worry and heartache. My mind clears while I float around the room with my eyes closed and let the tension of the last few days drain away. It isn't until the last chord fades that I look up to see I have an audience.

Sadie, Dare, and Justus stand by the door with smiles on their faces. I should've locked up before I began. Sadie rushes to me with her hands up. "Don't kill me. I talked to Dare, and I think you need to hear him out."

Sweat drips from my head as I walk over to grab a towel, and Sadie follows. "How long were you watching?"

"A few minutes."

Before I can respond, Dare grabs Justus's arm and drags him over to me. "Tell her," he growls.

Justus gives me an embarrassed grin. "Uh...yeah.

127

That wasn't Dare you heard at his apartment Friday night. It was me."

How stupid do they think I am? And why is Sadie buying their shit? "Nice try, but I heard her say Dare's name."

"Yeah." His pale face begins to flush. "I sort of told the woman my name was Dare."

My gaze jumps from Dare back to Justus. "And why would you do that?"

"Because I met her at a...um...party, and I didn't want her to be able to find me again. So, I gave her Dare's name and took her to his place."

Sadie gives me a terse nod from behind their backs. She believes them.

"If you don't believe him, I have a gas receipt in my car from a station in Ohio," Dare adds.

Sighing, I shake my head. "I believe you." I need to get away and process the information. I'm relieved it wasn't him, but my emotions are all over the place. "I'm going to shower. I'll...talk to you later," I tell Dare.

He scoffs and takes a seat. "I'm waiting right here. We need to talk."

Sadie tries to hide a smirk and grabs Justus's arm. "Let's go. You've done enough damage for one day."

"Damage! I saved the day!"

Sadie rolls her eyes. "This is the guy you were going to set me up with?"

"Sorry." I chuckle, shrugging.

"We don't need a set up. I'd love to take you out, sexy."

"Too late. I know your real name. It'd never work."

They continue their discussion while Sadie drags him outside.

I don't know what to say to Dare. I need to apologize since I accused him of something he didn't do, but that doesn't mean I'm going to jump back into bed with him. If there's one thing I've learned over the past few days, it's that I like him way too much. I've never been so jealous over a guy, and if I continue with him, I'm afraid I'm going to get hurt.

He approaches me, and his hands land on my hips. "You were beautiful out there. I didn't know you could dance like that."

"I didn't think anyone was watching." I peek up at him. "I'm sorry I accused you of lying and…screwing around. I realize it's none of my business who you're seeing. We didn't make any promises to each other."

"Bullshit. I said you were mine and I meant it. Maybe I need to make this a little clearer." His lips take mine, his hands cupping my cheeks, and he angles my face just right before slipping his tongue between my lips. His kiss is anything but gentle, and my hands fist in his hair as I give him back everything he's giving me.

His eyes are heated when we break apart. "You're mine, and I'll fight anyone who gets in my way. Understand?"

I've just been claimed by a kiss that left me speechless, and I've never been this turned on in my life, but I manage a response. "That goes for you too, then. No other women."

Sweeping me into his arms, he grabs my bag and heads for the door. "I don't need anyone else."

When I see where he's heading, I laugh. "Dare! I'm still in my leotard. I need to change."

"No way. I want you like this. Sexiest fucking thing I've ever seen."

He pauses for me to lock the door, but doesn't put me down. "My car," I point out when he puts me in his passenger seat.

"Justus can bring it. It's the least the fucker could do."

"You were so angry at him."

"Babe, you have no idea."

———

Dare rolls over and grins at me from my bed as I pull a sweater from the closet. "Are you going to the studio today?"

God, that man looks good in my bed. It's been three weeks since we officially got together. You'd think after spending every spare moment with him, I'd be accustomed to his gorgeous face and lickable body, but I'm still stunned by it, and the fact he's mine.

"No, no lessons today. Lisa closed the school. We got six inches of snow overnight."

"Perfect, I have an idea," he says, grabbing his phone.

Rather than listen in, I head to the shower. A glance in the mirror has me shaking my head. A small hickey resides on my neck, and a larger one on my breast. My chest and thighs are splotchy from the scruff on his face. This man is a monster, and I love every minute of it. I never used to go for the bad boy type, but damn I see the allure now.

Dare barges into the bathroom while I'm drying my

hair. He's fully dressed in dark jeans and a hoodie. "I have to go work with the guys for a few hours, but I want to take you somewhere when I get back."

"Where?"

"Suicide Hill." He grabs my hips and buries his nose in my hair, sniffing.

"Are we offing ourselves?"

"Fuck, you smell good. I have to get out of here before I take you again."

Giggling, I step back. "Focus, horndog. What's Suicide Hill?"

"It's a massive hill on a golf course. We've got plenty of snow for sledding, and it's not far away."

"You want to go sledding?"

"Well, tubing. Landon has a bunch of giant inner tubes in his garage. Zoe's going too, and maybe the rest of the guys. Bundle up and I'll pick you up around seven."

And bossy Dare is back. He really needs to learn to ask instead of ordering, but since I want to go, and he's excited, I'm not going to make an issue out of it. "Yes, sir," I reply, trying not to smile.

His palm meets my ass with a loud crack. "Keep up the backchat, baby, and you'll be calling me sir while you're over my knee." He massages my ass and gives me one of his long, slow kisses he knows drives me insane. A smile breaks across his face when a little moan escapes my lips, and he steps back. "Seven," he repeats, then strides out of the room.

I'm always off kilter with this man. He's unpredictable, soft when I expect hard, rough when I expect sweet. I love every minute of it. Of him. I'm falling fast and hard. It scares the shit out of me, but I don't care. I've never had a man treat me as well as he does, and I'm happier than I can ever remember being.

This is the point where I usually screw things up, or run. I spent a few months in therapy after the attack, and my therapist pointed out my habit of sabotaging my own happiness. Because everything I loved and wanted was taken from me so drastically, I'm always waiting for the other shoe to drop. It's like I'm afraid to be too happy or it'll be stolen away again. Not this time. I'm going with it and enjoying every second with him.

It'll be a few hours before he'll be back, and I consider inviting Sadie over, but I know she won't want to drive in snow if she doesn't have to. On impulse, I throw on my coat and walk across the street to Sunny's apartment, taking a container of chocolate chip cookies I made the night before.

Sunny and I always wave and say hi when we pass each other, but it's time I made an effort to talk to her. She's nice, and I need to make some new friends. Sunny opens the door, her face flushed, trying to catch her breath.

"Hey, did I come at a bad time?"

"No!" A wide smile appears on her face. "Come in. We just came in from playing in the snow."

Her little boy, Brody, struggles to get one of his boots off, and Sunny kneels in front of him, stripping off layers of clothes until he's only dressed in thermal under-clothes. He's nearly falling asleep on his feet. "Make yourself at home. I'll only be a second. Someone needs a nap."

"No nap," Brody protests, his eyes glassy.

"Yes, nap," Sunny tells him, carrying him down the hall.

We sit at her kitchen table when she returns, and she makes us each a cup of hot chocolate. "I thought you might like some company since we're trapped by snow."

"Absolutely. I don't know how a three-year-old can have more stamina than me, but he wears me out."

Sunny and I spend the next few hours laughing and chatting. Brody pronounces me his new best friend for bringing him cookies. When I'm getting ready to go, Sunny asks, "Are you still seeing that hunk of muscle that lives next door to you?"

"Yeah, he's picking me up in a bit to go sledding."

"I don't suppose he has a brother?"

"You aren't the first person to ask me that," I laugh. "But, he only has a younger sister."

We make plans to get together again, and I go home to pile on the clothes before Dare shows up.

When he knocks on my door just after dark, he's not alone. Justus walks in behind him, a wide smile on his face. "You ready, babe?" Dare asks.

"As I'll ever be. Do I want to know why it's called Suicide Hill?"

"Relax, no one has ever actually died."

"My buddy broke his collarbone last year," Justus says, like that's an accomplishment. "If you hit this one spot just right, you catch a lot of air."

"Good to know."

Dare grabs my hat while I'm slipping on my gloves and pulls it down over my ears, dropping a quick kiss on my lips. "I won't let you get hurt."

Justus tilts his head to the side and bats his eyelashes. "Aww, Dare is so sweet."

Dare glares at him, but when I laugh, his lips curl. "That's one," he growls.

"One what?" Justus laughs.

"You'll see."

After Dare unlocks his SUV, Justus hops in the front seat and pats his leg, signaling that I should ride on his lap. "Plenty of room," he says, winking at me.

Dare shoves him out the door and onto the snow covered ground, warning, "That's two."

Laughing, I step over him and slide into the passenger seat. Justus jumps up and brushes himself off before climbing into the back.

"Jeremy said he might show up, and Landon and Zoe are meeting us there," Dare tells me when we're finally on our way. The streets are still treacherous so there aren't many cars on the road. He steers us down a narrow back road and parks beside a tall fence.

His hand wraps around mine, and I'm led to a spot where the fence has been cut and peeled back. "Are we trespassing?" I ask.

"Along with about a hundred other people," he replies, chucking the inner tubes over the top of the fence. He's not far off. There are two massive hills across from each other and people are crowded at the top of them.

"Hey!" a voice shouts when we reach the top of the hill, and I see Jeremy, Landon, Zoe, and an unfamiliar redheaded woman smiling at us. Zoe waves, gesturing for us to join them.

"I was hoping you'd come!" Zoe exclaims. "This is my friend, Frannie."

Frannie and I exchange greetings, but I'm a little distracted by the guy standing beside Jeremy. He's looking at me like he knows me, but—holy shit.

"Tucker!" I barely recognize him. To be fair, he was usually dressed in shredded clothes with a scruffy beard and long hair when he lived in the parking lot. Now, he's clean shaven, his hair trimmed, and he's wearing dark jeans and a sweater.

"Ayda." He nods, a self-conscious smile on his face. "How have you been?"

"Good. You look great! How are you?"

Dare's arm slips around my shoulders, and Tucker smirks at him. "I'm fine, although I miss your cooking." He twists his hand, pointing his thumb at Dare. "Is this asshole treating you right?"

Dare scoffs and pulls me closer. "He's one of the good ones," I assure him. "Come by for dinner sometime."

"I sure will."

"Let's do this!" Justus shouts, flopping onto a tube. "Who's riding on my lap? Zoe? Ayda?" He turns to Frannie. "How about you? I love redheads."

Jeremy seat drops onto Justus's lap. Hard. Landon shoves the tube with his foot, sending them down the hill while everyone laughs.

"Jeremy is secretly in love with Frannie," Zoe tells me.

"Don't start that shit again," Frannie moans. "Fucking ain't love. We know the difference." She settles into another tube and pushes herself over the edge of the drop.

Zoe grins and shrugs when I look at her. "They have a love, hate, on again, off again thing."

Dare scoops me up from behind and sits down on the tube, settling me in his lap. "Ready, babe?"

He spins the tube around and shoves off, so we fly down the hill backward. Icy wind finds every crevice of my clothing, but it's totally worth it. Dare's warm arms stay around me while we fly down the hill, the quick drop tickling my stomach and making me laugh. The rest of the group is right behind us.

"Let's do it again!" I cry, jumping to my feet. Dare slips his arms around my waist and pulls me against him, grinning down at me.

"You're fucking adorable, you know that?"

My cheeks heat despite the bitter wind, and I look away.

His soft gloved hand lands on my cheek, making me look at him. He brings his lips to mine for a soft kiss. "Adorable," he repeats.

For the first time since the attack, I believe it. I don't know what it is, why this man can make me feel like there's nothing wrong with me when no one else could. When he looks at me, I don't worry that he's thinking about the scars, or disgusted by them. The way he gazes at me like he's a wolf and I'm his prey doesn't hurt. And the way his eyes darken when I'm laid out naked before him…"

"Keep looking at me like that, babe, and I can't be held responsible for my actions."

Shit. I'm standing here drooling over him. With a chuckle, he smacks my ass, then grabs my hand and heads back up the hill. "I've created a sex fiend."

"Pshh, I was a sex fiend way before you. I just haven't had a chance to act it out."

"I did used to hear your vibrator a lot."

"Shut up!" I smack his chest, and he laughs.

"Hang on," he says, dropping my hand and kneeling to scoop up a huge handful of snow. After packing it into a snowball, he turns and chucks it right into Justus's face, who's coming up the hill behind us.

Spluttering, Justus wipes his face. "What the hell?"

"That's one," Dare says. "Next one is coming when you least expect it."

We spend the next couple of hours at Suicide Hill, and I have a great time hanging out with Dare and his friends. I really like Zoe, and it's fun to watch Justus flirt and try to rile up the others. They tease and taunt each other, but you can see how close they all are. I'm happy to see Tucker become a part of their little group.

"We'll have to get together, go to the mall or something," Zoe suggests to me, as we all head back to the cars.

"I'd love to."

"I'll call you and we'll pick a day!" she calls, climbing into Landon's car.

"Sounds good!"

Justus rides home with one of the other guys, which leaves Dare and I alone in his SUV. "What's this dance competition you were talking about with Zoe?"

I rub my pink hands together in front of the heat vent. "It's a pretty big deal in the dance world. Nationally ranked dancers will be there, and one of the students I've been teaching is competing."

"When is it?"

"You want to go?" I ask, surprised.

"Would you rather I didn't?"

"No, I just...you don't seem like the type to like dance." A smile creases my face when I think of leading this huge tattooed man in to watch ballet.

His fingers slide between mine, and our hands rest on my thigh. "I like you."

CHAPTER
TEN

AYDA

Dare was disappointed when I told him I was going home for Christmas, and I know he was waiting on me to invite him, but there's no way I'd subject him to my mother. With a kiss and a promise to call, I leave early Christmas Eve.

Dread settles in the pit of my stomach when I start to pass the familiar landmarks of my childhood. It's not that my hometown of Lind, Ohio is terrible. It's a typical, middle sized Midwestern city, but the memories these streets bring back tear open wounds I thought were long healed.

My gaze soaks it up, taking in the small changes since I left. The small, family run café on the corner of Main Street is now a children's thrift store, one of the gas stations is closed down, another has been converted to a coffee shop. It's past eight p.m. Most of the stores and businesses are turning out their lights and locking their doors.

The Beauty of Dance Academy is still illuminated, the bright light pouring through the large plate glass windows. My car seems to park itself in front of the school. I haven't been through those doors since I was attacked, but I feel drawn to the place now.

Lena Sanger was my ballet teacher from the time I started at age eight until the day it was all taken from me. She was much more than a teacher to me, and I feel guilty for not staying in touch. When my mother—or rather her husband—decided my dance lessons were a waste of money and refused to pay, she let me continue anyway, completely free.

In fact, she used her own money to make sure I had the costumes and gear I needed to compete. She took me to the competitions and was the only one I had cheering me on. The last time I saw her was when she visited me in the burn unit of the hospital. I was less than thrilled to see her. I didn't want to see anyone, didn't want to hear them tell me everything would be okay when I knew nothing would ever be the same again.

The last students filter out the door, and I get out of the car before I can change my mind. The tiny bell on the door tinkles as I walk through, and Lena comes out of the dressing room to see who has entered. Her eyes nearly fall out of her head.

"Ayda?" She hasn't changed much. Lena was always a tiny woman, thin and petite like me, with a voice that could make a grown man stare at his toes while she chewed him out. Her hair has a bit more gray, and there are a few more lines on her face, but other than that, it's like I stepped back in time.

I feel like a teenager again when I give an awkward wave. "Hi."

A smile leaps to her face, and she wraps her arms around me, hugging me hard. "It's so good to see you! How are you? I asked your mom about you last week when I saw her in the bank."

Stepping back, I swallow the lump in my throat. I didn't realize how much I missed this woman until now. "I'm good. Really good. I'm sorry I haven't kept in touch, and I'm sorry for how I acted when you came to visit me."

She shakes her head. "Oh, honey, I never held that against you. It was a terrible time and you had to deal with it in your own way."

I gesture to the new coffee shop across the street. "Have a cup of coffee with me?"

"Of course! Just let me lock up."

Icy wind tries to slice us in half while we cross the road. It's a relief to duck inside the warm coffee shop which is redolent with the scent of coffee and baked goods. After ordering our drinks and a cinnamon roll each, we settle at a small table in the corner.

"How is Arnold?" I ask her. Arnold is her husband of over thirty years. I've met him a few times when he accompanied her to competitions.

She laughs. "Driving me crazy. He retired this year, and if he doesn't find a hobby other than yelling at football players on television, I'm going to choke him." Her eyes shine as she speaks, her love for him obvious.

"Now, tell me what you've been up to. Your mom said you're living in Indianapolis."

"I am. The physical therapy center they sent me to is located there. When I finished rehab, I decided it was a good place to start over. I work from home as a graphic artist, and give private dance lessons at a local school."

She grins at me and sips her coffee. "Husband? Boyfriend?"

"Boyfriend." I pull out my phone and bring up a picture of Dare. He was lying on my couch, shirtless, flipping through the TV channels when I snuck a photo.

She fans herself. "My goodness, girl, he's hot as a basted turkey."

"We haven't been together long, but we're happy."

Her hand wraps around mine. "I'm happy for you. How long are you in town?"

"For a couple of days. I'm here to visit my mom." My gaze meets hers, and I shrug. "I promised."

"Have you kept in touch with her?"

"We talk maybe once a month, but for some reason, she was insistent about me coming home at Christmas."

Lena's expression darkens. "I'm not trying to say anything negative about your family, hun, but you should know what you're walking into. There has been a lot of talk around town about Gil. He's been picked up twice for public intoxication. Darryl, the guy who works at the auto shop, found him passed out in the parking lot."

"I'd like to say I'm surprised, but it's about what I expected. I reserved a room at the Comfort Inn, so I can make a quick escape when I want to."

She nods and sits back in her seat. "Do you know your mom took a second job?"

Now, that's news I haven't heard, but I know why she didn't mention it. Gil won't hold a job since it interferes with his drinking and pill popping. She knows I'm not going to be nice about pointing that out. I've never understood why she lets him get away with the shit he does, but for as long as I can remember, her goal in life has been to give him whatever he wants. Nothing matters but Gil getting his way, no matter the damage it may cause to other people. It's been that way since they first met when I was ten.

"No, I didn't know. Where's she working?"

"Nights at the mower factory, mornings at the bakery." It probably makes me seem like the worst daughter in the world that I don't know what's going on in her life, but she's equally as clueless about mine. The truth is I don't want to know. The answer to the simplest question is always the same.

What is your mom doing these days?

Whatever Gil tells her to do.

It's sickening. I got tired of watching it and went my own way. It was the only good thing that came of what happened to me, being able to move to Indianapolis, far from all the bullshit. It gave me a chance to start over and find people who actually care about me.

Lena and I spend a few more minutes chatting. She catches me up on the local gossip before I reluctantly return to my car and start to my mom's house. Mom is pulling into the driveway, her fifteen year old sedan chugging and sputtering, and she climbs out holding a large paper bag from the liquor store.

A brand new car sits beside hers. Is someone else visiting?

I park behind her, and she waves when I climb out. "Ayda! You made it."

"I did." I gesture to the new car. "Is someone here? I don't want to block them in."

She flaps a hand at me. "No, that's Gil's car. Nice, isn't it?"

Gil—who doesn't do any work which doesn't involve tilting his elbow—has a brand new car while she's driving the POS to two jobs. "It's nice. Bet the insurance payments are a bitch," I remark.

She smiles, shaking her head. "Yeah, I started working mornings at the bakery to make up the difference."

There about a thousand things I want to say right now—or scream—but I know it won't do any good. The second I say anything negative about Gil, she'll lose her fucking mind and start screaming about how worthless and ungrateful I am. I just want to get through the next twenty-four hours and go home.

When I follow her inside, I'm glad I reserved a hotel room. Gil has always been a hoarder. In his mind, nothing is junk. He has to have it all, and nothing can ever be thrown away, but things have really escalated since I was here last.

There's barely a path through the living room to walk. Every inch of floor is piled with random junk, broken fishing poles, tools, busted small appliances. She leads me into the kitchen that smells of stale whiskey and old cheese. Half a bicycle rests against one wall, a stack of shoe boxes propping it up.

Gil lumbers out from the bedroom, his considerable gut leading the way, and grabs the bag from her hand. "About damn time."

"Sorry, we had to work over a little."

Grumbling, he makes his way back to the bedroom without acknowledging me, bottle in hand.

Merry fucking Christmas. Why did I come here again? I should be with Dare.

"Do you want something to eat or drink?" Mom asks.

"No thanks. I stopped on the way." Years of watching Gil scratch his nuts and pick his nose, then plunge his hands into the ice cube tray have taught me to avoid refreshments at their house.

"I was going to make a turkey dinner tomorrow, but I couldn't afford to get the ingredients." I don't doubt it, since every dime she makes goes to Gil's vices...and his new car.

"I was hoping to take you out to dinner tomorrow evening. Martha's is open and serving Christmas dinner."

Nervous eyes meet mine. "That sounds great. I'll have to see what Gil wants, though. He and Martha had a falling out years ago. He usually won't go there."

I'm at the end of my patience. "Then come without him. I'm only here until tomorrow night."

"I'll see. I'll talk him into it."

Talk him into letting her have dinner with her daughter on Christmas. I'm so disgusted. This isn't one of those typical situations where the timid little house-wife is afraid of her husband. He's not violent or abusive, just petulant and demanding, as dangerous as a typical three-year-old throwing a tantrum.

And she isn't weak. She proves that anytime anyone says something negative about Gil, and she attacks like a rabid dog. She loves him. Nothing and nobody else matters, including herself.

My head suddenly starts to ache, the smell of alcohol turning my stomach. "Claudia!" Gil bellows from the bedroom. "You took one of my Vicodin!"

"No, I didn't!" she screams back. She probably did. Mom doesn't drink, but pills have always been her thing.

"I had twelve, now there's eleven!"

"I'm going to go," I tell her. "I'll call you tomorrow about dinner."

"Okay, honey." She's barely listening, eager to get back to the bedroom and placate that idiot.

Walking out the front door, I feel nothing but relief. No matter how fucked up my life may have turned out, I'm not like her. No man will ever control my life.

Light snow flutters down, coating the ground while I make my way to one of the two hotels in this small town. A curse leaves my lips when I approach the desk. Terry Briggs is the night clerk. Every town has a busybody who's up on all the gossip, and Terry holds that honor here.

"Ayda! I heard you were coming to town to see your mama." Her eyes scan over the scars on my cheek, and the corners of her lips tuck in. "I was just remarking to Lettie the other day how you never come around. Was such a shame what happened to you. I've been praying for you."

Trying not to roll my eyes, I hand her my credit card. "Thanks. If I can just get my keycard."

"Of course! You must be tired after that drive. Heard

you moved to Indianapolis." She hands me the card, and I make a quick retreat down the hall. By tomorrow, half the town will know I'm here.

At least the room is clean and comfortable. I spend half an hour lounging in the tub, wishing I had never come here. I'll have dinner with Mom tomorrow, then go back home. My head still throbs when I crawl into bed, and my throat is starting to hurt. Great. I don't need to get sick right now.

My phone rings, and Dare's smirking face greets me. "Hey, babe. Did you make it okay?"

"Mmm hmm. Just crawled into bed. This place is deserted," I tell him with a chuckle.

"Your mom's house?"

"No, the Comfort Inn. Guess there's not a lot of demand on Christmas Eve."

"Why are you in a hotel? I thought you were visiting your family?"

Turning over, I sigh. "I can't stay with them. It's a long story. I don't feel very well right now, Dare. I'll call you in the morning, okay?"

"Are you sick?"

"Just a headache and a bit of a sore throat. It's no big deal. I'll call you when I wake up."

He agrees, but he doesn't sound happy about it. There's no time to worry about it, though, because my eyes slam shut the second my head hits the pillow.

Pounding on my door wakes me hours later. Who the hell? Someone must have the wrong room.

"Ayda! Open up. It's me. That bitch at the desk wouldn't give me a key."

Dare! The room spins a bit when I get to my feet too

quickly. I throw open the door and there he stands, a concerned expression on his face.

"What are you doing here?"

"Did you really think I was going to leave you alone, sick, on Christmas Eve?"

I throw my arms around him. "You crazy man! I'm fine, but I'm happy you're here."

His cheek presses to mine. "You're not fine. You're burning up. Let's get you in bed."

"That's what I'm talking about."

Laughing, he shakes his head and leads me back to bed. "You need to rest. I brought you some medicine."

I mentioned a headache and sore throat, and he drives three hours to bring me ibuprofen. He's too good to be true. "The twenty-four hour pharmacy was the only place open." He sits a bag on the bed and proceeds to unpack a few drinks, some snacks, and cold medicine. After handing me a couple of pills, he grabs a damp cloth from the bathroom and reclines beside me, placing the cool cloth on my forehead.

"You're going to miss the dinner at Landon's."

His strong arm wraps around me, and I lay my cheek against his cool chest. "I'm right where I'm supposed to be."

I'm right where I want to be.

"How did things go with your mom?"

"As expected." I can't keep the resignation out of my voice. I didn't expect anything to have changed, so I'm not sure why I feel disappointed. It's not like I thought she'd be thrilled to see me, but she's the one who insisted I had to come visit for Christmas. "I don't know why she wanted me to come," I confess.

"She's your mom. Whatever issues you two have, I'm sure she misses you."

There's no point in arguing. He doesn't know her. Hopefully, he never will. "I'm glad you're here."

He kisses my head, and I snuggle into him. The nighttime cold medicine drags my eyes shut. "Good night, Dare."

"Good night, Ayda."

———

Martha's Country Cookin' is a family owned restaurant that's been open since before I was born. Every Thanksgiving and Christmas they offer a huge buffet, and it seems like half the town has decided to eat here instead of cooking.

Dare pulls my chair out, and I take a seat, gnawing on my lip. I didn't want him to come, but I couldn't leave him at the hotel after he cancelled his plans and came all this way for me. Mom is sure to do something to embarrass me, and god help us if she brings Gil.

"Relax, everything will be fine. We'll have dinner, then head back to Indy," he assures me.

"Just eat fast," I mumble, and he laughs. I feel much better today, the fever is gone and my throat has gone from sore to scratchy, but I'm still a bit worn down. I'm ready to get this over with.

Mom walks in, stopping to chat with a few people on her way to our table, and I breathe a sigh of relief that Gil isn't with her. "I hope you weren't waiting long," she says, then turns to me. "Ayda, you didn't tell me you were bringing a friend."

"Derek," Dare says before I can reply. He gets to his feet and extends his hand. "Ayda's boyfriend. It's nice to meet you."

Hell, she could at least try not to look so shocked. I mean, I get it. Dare looks like he walked off of a fitness magazine and half my face looks like crinkled paper, but she could pretend.

"Nice to meet you too."

Not much else is said while we fill our plates and sit down to eat. The food is good at least, and I start to relax a little. Maybe we'll get through dinner without any drama.

Mom dominates the conversation with gossip about my old friends and neighbors. And Gil, of course. Gil likes this. Gil doesn't like that. Gil thinks politics is a waste of time. Blah Blah Blah.

Dare gives me a little half grin and winks. "How are you feeling, babe?" He turns to Mom. "She was sick last night."

Mom looks up. "Oh? Gil was sick last week. Stomach flu."

My shoulders lift in a shrug when Dare looks at me. It's pointless. "I'm feeling better. I think I'm going to grab a bowl of that banana pudding."

"Let me get it. I've been eyeing the chocolate cake," he volunteers, dropping a kiss on my head before starting away. I love how he does that, kisses my head or forehead whenever he leaves.

Mom turns to me the second he walks away. "I was hoping to get a second alone with you." She sits back in her chair and sighs. "Things have been really tough lately, and I know you got that settlement money from

Talbot. Since you've sworn not to touch it, I could really use a few thousand to get us through the winter."

I should've known. This is the reason she wanted me to come home. She wants money. Dare returns to the table, his forehead creasing at the thick tension now surrounding us.

"Your mortgage is paid off, and I paid this year's property taxes. What's behind?" I ask, not hiding my exasperation.

Her glare attempts to slice me in half, but I don't care. I'm not giving her money to fund Gil's drinking and shopping. "I'm asking you for help, and you want what? An itemized list?" she hisses.

"Preferably one that doesn't mention Gil."

"He's been like a father to you!"

That's it. I'm done. "If you want to spend your life worshipping at the feet of a drunk, narcissistic asshole, that's your choice. I want no part of it, and he's certainly not living off of my money." I get to my feet, and Dare silently accompanies me. "When you're ready to throw his worthless ass out, call me, and I'll help you any way you need. But you can forget about the settlement money. I gave it to charity."

Her face burns bright red, and she shouts across the crowded restaurant as we walk away. "This is why no one can love you! You aren't just ugly on the outside, but to the bone!"

Dare stops cold and turns, his eyes blazing.

Shit.

I squeeze his hand and look him in the eye. "Let's go, please. I don't feel well, and it's nothing I haven't heard before. Nothing all these people haven't heard before," I mumble. "Just get me out of here."

He wraps his arm around me so tightly that it's hard to breathe and walks me out to his car. Silence fills the small space on our drive back to the hotel. His anger is palpable, hanging in the air around us.

Once we're back in our room, I flop onto the bed, exhausted. "I'm sorry. I tried to get you not to come with me."

"You're sorry?" His hands run through his hair. He sits beside me and pinches my chin between his fingers, making me look at him. "You don't have one damn thing to be sorry about."

CHAPTER
ELEVEN

DARE

I've never wanted to hit a woman until Ayda's mother screamed across that restaurant. What pissed me off even more was the expression on Ayda's face. There was no surprise or hurt, just resignation. Like having her mother scream that she's ugly and no one can love her is an everyday occurrence. Fuck, maybe it was.

Her eyes gaze into mine as we sit on the edge of the hotel bed. "What was that about?" I ask softly, and she sighs.

"Her husband has managed to spend all her money. Now she expects me to let him have mine."

"No offense, Ayda, but you aren't exactly raking in the cash. What makes her think you can afford to give her money? What was the settlement you mentioned?"

Ayda kicks off her shoes and scoots up the bed until she's leaning against the headboard. "First, you need to understand that it doesn't matter to her whether I have the money. Her tunnel vision is only focused on one thing. Give Gil what he wants. And the settlement money, well, I lied. I didn't give it to charity. I dumped it into an account and left it there. It's nothing but a payoff."

Her brow creases. "I lost everything. My looks, a career in dancing that I worked for since I was a child, everything. Two-hundred thousand dollars was what my future was worth. I didn't want his daddy's fucking money. I wanted him to pay for what he did to me."

Her body stiffens before relaxing into mine when I pull her into my arms. "You didn't lose your looks. You're beautiful, and you're a beautiful dancer. I'm sorry he ruined your career. And trust me, he's going to pay for the pain he's put you through."

I thread my fingers into her soft hair, gripping it and tilting her head until I'm met with those defeated eyes. "You amaze me. You are the strongest woman I've ever met in my life. Even after all that's happened to you, you haven't hardened against people, or lost your ability to empathize. The kindness you showed to Tucker when the rest of us walked past him without a glance demonstrated that."

She shrugs. "I know what it's like to be invisible, or worse, to be gaped at like a circus animal. I keep my head down. I guess that allows me to see others on my level."

"There are no levels, but fuck, babe, if there were you'd be miles above the rest. Miles above me," I murmur. It's not the first time the thought has occurred to me. She deserves better than me, better than an ex-con still involved in criminal activities. I don't doubt what I do is necessary and for the greater good, but it could still land me back in prison.

"That's not true," she argues, cuddling against me.

"There's a lot you don't know about me. I don't want to scare you away, but you should know what you're getting into."

The gravity of my voice makes her sit up, her gaze wary. "You aren't married or anything, are you?"

"No. There's no one else but you. You're the first woman I've dated for over four years."

Her lips tuck in. "I heard other women in your apartment. Not that it's any of my business, but you don't have to lie."

"I'm not lying. I'm about to give you more truth than you probably want, and maybe I shouldn't considering the night you've had, but not telling you is starting to seem like lying, and I don't want to lie to you."

"Okay, I'm ready."

I wish I was. "Yes, you heard other women, but they were one night stands. I've never been the playboy type, but after three years in prison, I needed something, and they filled the gap."

Her eyes widen, and she starts picking at a fingernail. "Prison?"

"Yes, I got out almost a year ago."

"What did you do time for?" she whispers.

"I was charged with attempted murder, but they convicted me on the lesser charge of aggravated assault."

She falls silent for a moment, processing the information. Her knees draw up, and she wraps her arms around them. The distance between us suddenly feels like The

Grand Canyon, and the thought she's now afraid of me twists my stomach.

"What did you do?"

"My kid sister came to me when she was in her senior year of high school and told me what had been happening to her. Our uncle had been molesting her, raping her, for years." I stumble over the words and have to cough to clear my throat. "Since she was a little girl."

A soft hand climbs into mine while I continue. I'm not really seeing the off white walls around me anymore, my mind is focused on that spring day that changed everything. "I've never been so angry, before or since, and there was nothing anyone could've done to stop me from giving that sick bastard what he had coming. I beat him until the cops showed up and pulled me off him."

There are things I can't tell her, things that are mine to keep. The way the grass turned crimson with the man's blood, how it sprayed into my face and splashed my clothes, the sound of crunching, breaking bone beneath my fists. But most of all, she can never know the only part I do feel shame about. How much I enjoyed it, his screams and pleading cries.

How many times had my sister begged him to stop, only to be ignored and tortured? Her tear streaked face was all I could see. Every punch and resulting shriek felt like a victory for her. I hate it that I have that kind of violence in me, and that I'm capable of enjoying it, but I don't regret what I did. Even if he'd died, I would still know I did what I could for her, even if it was too little, too late.

"You didn't kill him," she says, and I'm not sure if it's a question or a reassurance.

"No, but not for lack of trying. I paralyzed him."

Her soft legs are warm against mine as she straddles my lap and lays her hands on my shoulders. "You were protecting your family. You shouldn't have gone to prison for that."

"You can't take the law into your own hands and not face the consequences. I knew what would happen to me, but I didn't care."

"Because you were doing the right thing," she says, before dropping a soft kiss on my lips.

I hope she believes that. "There's more. I need you to understand that I'm not only putting myself at risk by telling you this. Even if you never want to see me again, I need you to swear you'll keep this secret."

"You can trust me."

I run my hand through her hair, watching it slip through my fingers, hoping she doesn't do the same. "I know. I wouldn't be telling you otherwise. I told you I worked in internet security."

"Yeah."

"It wasn't a lie, but it's not the complete truth either. I use my computer skills to keep kids safe. I work with a group who specialize in hunting down and tracking online predators and pedophiles."

"And bring them to justice?" I know what she's asking.

"Most of the time, yes, we hand the information over to the police, anonymously, but not always. Too many of them beat the system. They keep letting them out again and again, as if putting them on a list will keep them from victimizing another child." My eyes meet hers. "It doesn't."

Picking her nail again, she asks, "But you do?"

"My group does. If they keep targeting kids and get away with it, we make them disappear."

"You kill them," she says, clarifying.

"Yes. My part is typically limited to tracking and gathering information, but if we're ever caught, I'll be just as culpable."

Silence has never felt this heavy. I want to know what's going through her head right now, but I know she needs a second to process everything. There's only one thing I need her to know. "I'd never hurt you, Ayda. I'd never hurt a woman. I've never hurt anyone who wasn't a predator."

Her features soften as she gazes at me. "I know that."

"You can ask me whatever you want. Say whatever you want. I won't get upset."

I try to prepare myself for anything. For her to start getting dressed to leave, or ask me to go, but what I get is more than I dared to hope for.

"I don't want you to go back to prison."

A chuckle of relief escapes, and I lie back, pulling her onto my chest. "Neither do I."

"But you could. You could get caught. If someone finds a body…"

"The bodies are…they don't exist anymore. They can't be found. We're careful. Extremely careful. Outside the group, Zoe is the only one who knows the truth about ISH."

"ISH?"

"In Safe Hands. It's what we call ourselves."

"I like it," she says, like she's judging wallpaper or something.

158

"It's okay to be freaked out."

She rolls onto her side and props her head on her hand. "I guess I should be, huh?"

"But you're not?"

"The world is a fucked up place, and life isn't fair. I know that from experience. You're trying to make it better, safer, at a humongous risk to yourself. I'd say it's noble if I didn't think it'd make your head even bigger."

"You're something else, Ayda Brooks."

"Besides, it goes well with my side job as a bounty hunter slash vigilante."

Laughing, I play with her hair. I've never cared about a girl's hair before, but my fingers can't seem to resist hers. "Yeah, do you take down the bad guys with your ballet moves?"

"Then I tie them up with my leotards." She peeks up at me and dissolves into giggles. "Would it be weird if I said this has been the best Christmas I've had in a long time?"

"Me too, babe. Me too."

———

Ayda knows everything and she didn't run away screaming. Saying I feel relieved would be a huge under-statement. I talked to the guys, prepared to deal with their anger since I didn't exactly get their okay to tell her about ISH, but they aren't concerned. I trust her, so they trust her.

The dance competition is today. Holding Ayda's small, soft hand in mine, I let her lead me into a sea of pastel hell. Leotard and tutu clad children and adults are everywhere, stretching and warming up.

"Wait here, I'll be right back," Ayda says, disappearing into one of the dressing rooms.

I get a few wary looks, but I'm not surprised. I stick out like a dick on a cake among all these dainty, graceful people. She returns with a boy in tow. A man I assume must be his father follows them.

"I'll be right there in the front row beside Ms. Lisa," she tells him, pointing to a few empty seats. "You're going to be amazing."

His face is tight as he nods, forcing a smile. "I've got this."

"Yes, you do." She gives him a quick hug, then shows me to our seats.

"Hey, Lisa," she greets the woman in the seat beside us. "Ryan's pretty nervous."

The woman smiles and shakes her head. "I know, but he'll be fine once he gets started. I have a sixteen-year-old student who looks like she's going to puke any minute. If anyone is going to lose it or freeze up, it'll be her."

"We've all been there." When Lisa smiles at me, Ayda exclaims, "Oh, sorry, I'm being rude. Dare, this is Lisa. She owns the dance studio where I've been giving lessons. Lisa, this is Dare, my boyfriend."

After we exchange pleasantries, she regards Ayda. "Woman, where have you been hiding this guy?"

Ayda laughs, a cute blush pinking her cheeks. "I like to keep him to myself."

"I don't blame you." She grins at me. "Do you have any brothers?"

Ayda laughs aloud as I shake my head. "You're the third person to ask that," Ayda tells her.

Lisa turns to talk to someone on her other side, and I slide my arm around Ayda's shoulder, settling back in my seat. "Who else asked?"

She rolls her eyes. "Like I need to make your head any bigger."

"It only gets big for you, babe."

The audience quiets when the first dancer takes her place on stage. I came today for Ayda, as a show of support, and I didn't expect to enjoy the experience. But these kids are amazing. It's not all boring ballet numbers set to classical music like I expected. There are teams doing hip hop and routines that tell a story, which Ayda tells me is called Lyrical.

The boy Ayda has been teaching finally takes the stage, and she grabs my hand, crushing it in hers. She's surprisingly strong. I don't think she takes a breath through his entire routine. Her eyes are bright and excited, and she murmurs to herself. In her mind, she's up there with him through every step, jump, and turn, living it with him, as invested in his success as his parents.

The passion and love she feels for dance glows on her face, and I can almost feel her yearning to be the one gliding across that stage. I wish I could've seen her then. Her hand relaxes a little in mine when his performance is over, but tightens again when they announce the winners.

"Yes!" she cries, turning to hug Lisa, and then me when he wins in his division.

Ayda grabs my hand, and I accompany them backstage where she wraps Ryan in a bear hug. "I knew you could do it!"

His face is flushed with joy as his dad follows suit, hugging and congratulating him. Ayda is in her element here, laughing and talking with the dancers and parents backstage, happier than I have ever seen her.

Her eyes suddenly darken, and she takes my hand. "I'm ready to go, okay?" She pulls me toward the exit.

"Hey." She pauses reluctantly when I stop. "What's wrong?"

"Nothing," she mumbles, glancing behind me. "I just want to get out of here."

"Our coats are in the dressing room. I'll grab them."

"I'll be at the stage door." Releasing my hand, she rushes off.

What the hell was that? Ayda can be a bit eccentric sometimes, it's part of her charm, but something obviously freaked her out. It's not until I grab our coats and make my way toward the door that I understand. Victoria Towne stands backstage, watching the dancers who are still competing.

This is the woman who stole Ayda's chance to be a professional dancer. The bitch who got her boyfriend to throw acid in her face and got away with it. Fear streaks through me. If she's here, Talbot may be as well. As much as I want to confront the woman, Ayda's safety is my priority, and my heart plummets when I see she isn't waiting at the stage door.

I open the door and red blankets my vision. Talbot stands across from Ayda, wearing a hateful grin. She backs away from him, her face as white as the snow on the ground, her hands rubbing her bare arms for warmth. "Get away from me!"

"Like I want to touch you," he sneers. "God, I really fucked you up, didn't I? Not even a mother could love that face."

Her wince makes him smile. He has no idea how close to the bone that hit. There's no one else in the alley to see what I'm about to do, but I wouldn't care if there was. The fear in her eyes tears a chunk from my heart, and I'm going to make sure she never has to be afraid again.

"Dare! No!" she calls when I slam my fist into his jaw, but I barely hear her. My ears are filled with the sound of rushing blood, and his jeering voice gloating over what he did to her. I don't feel the cold or the one punch he manages to land before I get him to the ground and start pounding his face. I'm not trying to kill him, but I won't be satisfied until his face bears scars as well as hers. Since I don't have any acid handy, I do the best I can with my fists.

He gives up trying to hit me and instead uses his hands to block his face while attempting to roll over, but he isn't getting me off him. Straddling his chest, I throw punch after punch, breaking his jaw and sending teeth skittering across the pavement. This isn't like when I beat up my uncle. I'm not blind with rage, and I can aim my punches where they'll do the worst damage.

"Oh my God!" a female voice screams. "He's killing him! Call the police!"

A few seconds later, sirens ring out from a distance and Ayda's pleading reaches my ears. "The cops are coming, Dare! Please!"

Finally, I get to my feet, leaving the now unconscious Talbot bleeding on the pavement, his face resembling ground beef. Victoria must've been the one who screamed about police. She's standing outside the stage door in a leotard and skirt, tears pouring down her face. She flinches as I regard her. "Say one fucking word to Ayda or come near her again and your face will match his."

The only other person present is Lisa, who urges me to run, but I know better. I beat a guy half to death... again. I don't need evading tacked on to the charges I'm sure to face. "Make sure Ayda gets home okay."

Lisa nods, and Ayda throws her arms around me. "I'm sorry, babe, but I had to."

"H-how did you know it was him?" she stammers.

Shit. There's no quick answer for that since I haven't told her I've been cyber-stalking her attackers. "I'll explain later. I need you to call Landon and tell him what happened." I hand her my phone and car keys. "The password is Ayda. Now, stay back," I order when the first officer arrives on the scene. "Everything will be all right."

I hope she can't hear the lie in my voice.

CHAPTER
TWELVE

AYDA

This can't be happening, but there's no denying what my eyes are telling me. Dare sits in the back of the squad car, his hands cuffed behind him while the cop receives very different statements from Lisa and Victoria. Lisa approaches me before the cop can question me and hisses, "Talbot swung first. He followed you out here and grabbed you. Dare was defending you." There was no need to remind me since I heard Dare tell the officer the same thing.

I nod and wipe the tears rolling down my face at the sight of Dare headed back to jail because of me. An ambulance scoops up a moaning Talbot from the street and carts him away, siren blaring, while I lie to a cop for the first time in my life.

After taking all our information, he returns to his car and drives away, taking the only man I've ever loved with him. It's a hell of a time for such a realization, but I can't deny it's true. I'm in love with Dare. And now, it could be years before I see him again.

"Do you need a ride home?" Lisa asks softly.

"No, go back in and tend to your dancers. I'm fine. I'm sorry this happened here, Lisa." She took a chance on me, and I brought this mess to her door in the middle of a competition.

Her lips thin, and she glares at Victoria, who quickly retreats inside. "It isn't your fault. I didn't know she'd be here, but apparently they invited her to do an exhibition solo." A grin tilts her lips when she faces me. "You've got a good man there, Ayda. Don't blame him. That guy had it coming."

"I know. I have to go and let his friend know, probably call a lawyer."

"Be careful and call me later." She gives me a quick hug then heads back inside, stepping around the blood on the ground.

Shivering, I make my way home in Dare's car, not even thinking to turn on the heat. As soon as I get in my apartment, I enter my name in his phone to unlock it, and tears well up again at the sight of his wallpaper. It's a picture of me, asleep with my curls spread across the pillow. When did he take that?

Landon answers on the second ring and assures me he'll handle everything. "There's nothing you need to do," he assures me. "I'll get the lawyers on it and see if Mason can intervene." I have no idea who he's talking about, but I don't want to keep him on the phone. Every second he spends talking to me is time better spent helping Dare.

When I hang up, silence closes in around me, and I pace the apartment. I'm tempted to call Sadie, but there's too much I can't tell her. I don't know what to do with myself, and I have to fight the urge to call Landon back and demand to know what's going on.

Oh hell. Has it really only been an hour? I'm never going to make it through this night.

It started out so well. My life has been getting better and better. Like a recurring nightmare, Talbot and Vicky show up to destroy everything again. This time it isn't only me they're screwing with, and I can't let them fuck up Dare's life too.

My heart leaps at the sound of a knock on my door. I expect Landon, but it's Zoe who walks through the door. One look at my face and she wraps me in a hug. "I thought you might need some company."

"Do you know what's going on?" We take a seat on the couch.

"Landon's meeting with Mason and the lawyer. They expect Talbot to press charges, and they're hoping to get Dare out on bail in the meantime. With his record, it might be hard."

"Who is Mason?"

"Mason Reed. He and his brothers run a domestic violence shelter for women and children called Striking Back. He's a powerful guy, with judges and cops on his side. ISH and Striking Back often help each other. If anyone can dig Dare out of this mess, it's Mason."

"So, all we can do is wait," I remark, laying my head back and closing my eyes.

"Pretty much. I'm sure Mason and Landon are dragging judges out of bed as we speak. We should know something soon. In the meantime..." Zoe produces a bottle of wine from her bag. "Let's have a glass and watch a movie, try to keep our minds occupied."

It's nearly dawn when Zoe leaves. "Landon should be getting home. He can't be out in the daylight."

"Dare mentioned that, some kind of condition that makes him burn instantly in the sun?"

"Yeah, I hate it for him, but he handles it well."

I give her a hug. "Thanks for coming."

"Get some sleep. I'm sure we'll know something today."

Confident that I won't sleep a wink, I stretch out on the couch, keeping my phone nearby in case Landon calls. The wine and the extremely long day overwhelm the worry and anxiety pulsing in my brain, knocking me out almost instantly.

Shouting wakes me late in the afternoon. "I said I'd get her! Fuck! Go clean the sand out of your vagina!"

Rolling off the couch, I jerk open my apartment door to see Justus, his fist raised to knock. "Hey, tiny dancer. Will you please get next door before Dare completely loses his shit?"

"He's home!" I turn and grab my coat, rushing out behind Justus. "What happened? They let him go?"

Justus grins and shakes his head. "I'll let him explain."

Dare pulls me into his arms as soon as I'm through the door. "Are you okay?"

"Shouldn't I be asking you that?" I'm so relieved to see he's all right.

"Has anyone tried to contact you? Talbot? His father?"

Confused, I step back. "I doubt Talbot's talking to anyone since you broke his jaw. And why would his dad? What's going on, Dare? How did you even know who he was? I never told you who hurt me."

Justus retreats to the door. "Yeah, I'm going to let you two sort this out. Call me if you need anything, Rockem Sockem."

Dare doesn't seem to hear him. His hand runs through my hair. "Let me get a shower and I'll explain everything, okay?" He looks exhausted. I can't imagine a night in jail is pleasant.

"I'll make you something to eat," I volunteer before bringing my lips to his. Tension drains from him, his shoulders relaxing as our lips and tongues soothe each other, washing away the events of the last twenty-four hours.

He leans his forehead against mine with a sigh.

"Everything will be okay," I murmur, and he nods. We both know I'm lying. We have no way of knowing how things are going to turn out, but for the moment, we can pretend.

His fridge is only stocked with beer, water, and condiments. Typical. I run next door to grab a container of chili from my freezer, a box of cornmeal mix, and a quart of milk. If there's one thing I've learned from living alone, it's to freeze your leftovers if you don't want to be stuck eating the same thing for days to prevent them from spoiling. It occurs to me while I'm juggling everything and trying to open the door that it would've been easier to have him come to my place.

The chili is heating on the stove, and the cornbread is in the oven when he returns, rubbing his hair with a towel. The warm, clean smell of steam and soap drifts through the apartment. "What are you making? It smells fantastic."

"Chili and cornbread. Do you ever keep food in your place?"

A noise escapes his chest, a cross between a huff and a laugh. "I will be now." Sitting at his small kitchen table, he hikes up the leg of his sweat pants, displaying the tracking anklet fastened around his ankle.

"Oh. House arrest? For how long?"

"Until the trial."

The chair scrapes the floor as I sit across from him and lean my chin on my hand. "I'm sorry, Dare. I never would've had you come if I knew there was going to be trouble."

He blinks, surprised. "I beat the shit out of a guy and you're apologizing?"

"You're in trouble because of me. Big trouble."

His hand darts across and grabs mine. "First, you didn't tell me to kick that psycho's ass. I got myself in trouble. And second, I'd do it again."

The timer beeps, and I busy myself doling out bowls of chili with slices of cornbread. Dare grabs two bottles of water and sits down across from me. He tears into the food like he hasn't eaten in a week while I pick at mine.

Dare sighs and glances at me. "I've been watching them."

"What?" My elbow bumps my water bottle, and I catch it just in time.

"Talbot and his father. Victoria to a lesser extent."

My mind is stuffed with questions. "What do you mean watching? And how did you know who to watch?"

Leaning back in his chair, he gazes at me. "It wasn't hard to find an article online about your attack, babe. Montgomery did a good job of burying everything, but not good enough. Once I had Talbot's name, it wasn't hard to figure out the rest."

"But...why?"

"Because they hurt you and they need to pay for it. I learned a lot more once I started digging around. Those two should be the ones in prison."

"You should've told me."

"I know. I didn't want you to get involved. Nothing I did will ever get traced back to me."

My eyes dart up to meet his. "What did you do?"

A small grin creeps across his face. "Victoria may have some financial trouble coming."

"What did you do? Charge up her credit card?"

"I might have maxed them out, plus a few she doesn't know she applied for. She also has recently borrowed a whopping amount of money from different lenders and cash advance companies."

Maybe I'm evil, but I can't help the joy I feel knowing she's getting some kind of payback, no matter how trivial. People say revenge isn't the answer, but it feels a fuck of a lot better than the alternative.

"Where did the borrowed money go?"

"Random charities."

"And Talbot and Montgomery?"

"I'm still looking into them. Playing the long game." He squeezes my hand. "I don't want you to worry about any of this, Ayda. I've got it handled."

"Don't get yourself in any more trouble over my problems."

His grin tells me he has no intention of agreeing to that. "Let's just hang out tonight, okay? I want to watch TV with you, then fuck you until we both forget everything."

"What about your ankle tracker? How far can you go?"

"Can't even step out the damn front door. I was hoping my beautiful neighbor would get my mail for me."

"You tell that bitch that's my job."

Dare puts our dishes in the dishwasher, then pulls me into his living room. We snuggle on the couch, his bulging arms holding me close. "You're going to need more than your mail, you know. If you can't leave the house, you need groceries and stuff."

"I just need you." A rush of warmth spreads through me, and the words fall from my lips before I can stop them.

"I love you." Instant regret fills me, and I scramble to sit up. "I'm sorry, you don't have to say it back, it... slipped out. It doesn't have to mean anything," I babble. After all this I'm going to lose him from dropping the L bomb on him too early.

Soft lips find mine in a firm kiss as I'm pulled back and rolled underneath him. His wide body barely fits on the couch, and the pressure of his weight on me feels amazing. When we break apart, his eyes sear into mine. "It means everything."

He doesn't say it back, but he shows it in every tender, affectionate kiss left on my skin. We don't last long on the couch before he scoops me up and carries me to the bedroom for hours of sheet clawing, mind numbing sex.

I don't care that he's a criminal.

I don't care that he didn't tell me he was researching my past.

I don't care about anything but being with this hard man who softens at my touch.

———

As the days wear on, being cooped up inside takes a toll on Dare. Though he does his best not to take it out on me, he wants me with him every minute. He's bored and not accustomed to being alone, so I bring my laptop to his place to work on my graphic art projects. I also run his errands when I do mine. It's the least I can do for the guy who beat the shit out of my attacker.

He's still working on something when it comes to Talbot and Montgomery, but he never gives me a straight answer. Eventually, I quit asking. If it's hacker stuff, I probably wouldn't understand anyway. I'll just have to trust him.

"I'm working at the studio tonight," I tell him. "I'll be back late."

Looking up from his computer, he gives me one of his devastating smiles. "I want you naked as soon as you come through the door."

"I could always strip in the parking lot and make it quicker," I tease.

Stalking over to me, he backs me up against the wall, his hand slipping behind me to squeeze my ass. "Nobody sees this body but me." I tilt my head, giving him access to my neck, and let out a moan when he takes advantage, sucking and licking. My neck has always been my weak spot and it didn't take him long to capitalize on it.

His huge palm slips between my legs, caressing me. "This is mine."

"Mmm." That's not enough of an agreement for him.

"Say it, babe."

God, if he keeps massaging me like that I'll never get out of here. "My body is yours." I reach down to stroke the hard-on being held back by only a pair of sweat pants. "And this is mine." He groans and thrusts his hips forward.

"But," I add, stepping away, my voice light and teasing. "I have to go, so you have my permission to play with it while I'm gone."

I'm out the door before he can grab me, and he chuckles, shaking his head. "You'll pay for that later."

"Looking forward to it."

I feel sorry for him when he closes the door. Being trapped at home sucks, but there's nothing we can do, and it could be much worse. All this time we're spending together, I know he wants it for the same reason I do, because we may not have much time left. He could be taken away from me for years.

It's too painful to think about, and I'm happy to retreat to the studio where I can lose myself to the music. It's late when I finish my last lesson with a pre-teen girl, and the school is empty after she leaves with her mother. I'm turning off the lights when I hear the front door open and close. I need to remember to lock it behind my last student.

Sliding my coat on, I walk to the lobby, expecting to see a student who has forgotten something, or maybe Lisa coming back to work on the books. The lobby is empty. That's weird. Maybe someone opened the door, then walked back out? There's no way they made it past the lobby without me seeing them.

My voice bounces back, echoing down the hall when I call out, but no one answers. I'm getting a little creeped out, but it's probably from being alone in a dark place that's usually filled with light and life. Scooping the keys from the counter, I make my way toward the door, smiling when my thoughts turn to Dare and what he's promised to do to me when I get home. He's turned me into a sex fiend.

The room shifts, and a croak escapes my throat as I try to draw a breath. Fingers tighten around my neck, and I'm suddenly on the floor with no idea how I got there. I'm pinned, a heavy body on top of mine. "Not one fucking word, you ugly bitch, you hear me? Don't say one fucking word."

Talbot. A flash of headlights through the windows briefly illuminates his face. No wonder I didn't recognize his voice. His jaw is wired shut, and he's talking in a mumble that's hard to understand. Fading bruises stain his cheeks and forehead.

My chest is on fire, my lungs crying out for oxygen, and the room starts to look watery. He loosens his grasp, and I pull a painful lungful of air, then another, terrified at how close I just came to never breathing again.

"Look at me. Are you listening to me, bitch?" Spittle flies out of his mouth in a fine spray, landing on my face.

When I nod frantically, he smiles, and there isn't an

ounce of sanity in it. "Good. I could have your boyfriend locked up until you're both old and gray, you know that? It's all up to me. If I don't show up to court, the case gets tossed like nothing ever happened. So, let me tell you how this is going to go. You're going to stay the fuck away from him."

Why does he give a shit who I'm with? "W-why?"

His palm connects with my face, splitting the edge of my lip. "Because I fucking said so! You fuck up everything. From now on, you don't get to have shit unless I say so. That includes your neighbor. If I see you together, I'll get my father involved. He'll spend the next ten years behind walls. Do what I say, and I'll forget to be in court that day. Understand?"

These aren't empty threats. He's fucking crazy. "Yes," I whisper.

"Remember, I'll be watching." With a chuckle, he gets off me and walks away humming *I'll Be Watching You* by The Police.

Dare wasn't the only one spying. How else would Talbot know he's my neighbor? My throat burns as I stumble to the door to turn the lock after he leaves. My mind races and dizziness washes over me. With my back to the wall, I slide down to sit on the floor, my head in my hands. I thought all of this was behind me. Victoria, Talbot, his father. They haven't bothered me for years. I moved away. I thought I got away.

Why does he want to hurt me now? Back then, he did it to get his girlfriend the scholarship that I won, but I have nothing she wants now. Is it as simple as revenge?

If he and Dare had never crossed paths, this never would've happened. Now, I don't know what to do. I love Dare. I'm so in love with him, and I can't imagine my life without him now. Even though he hasn't said it, I know he loves me too. Either I break both of our hearts, or risk Dare going back to prison. I can't do that to him. It's better to end things now, maybe get him off the Coulter's radar while he still has a chance.

Dare breaks the law every day, but he does it to help children. No matter how well ISH covers their tracks, a senator looking into them could blow apart the whole operation, send them all to jail, and leave the children they're helping unprotected.

There's no real decision to be made here. I have to love him enough to keep him away from me, so he isn't brought down by the same monster who ruined me. Curled up in a ball, I don't know how long I sit on that floor, grieving what Dare doesn't even realize we've lost. Worse, there's no way to end our relationship in person. I don't doubt for a second Talbot or one of his minions is watching.

My phone dings with a text message from Dare.

Dare: Are you running late?

I don't know what to do. I can't tell him the truth. He'll go after Talbot and get himself locked up again.

Me: I'm staying at a friend's house tonight. Don't wait for me.

I should tell him we're over, but I can't make myself type the words. I also can't go home. I can't bear him trying to talk to me through the walls, or even breaking his house arrest to come get me.

My phone rings, and Dare's face smiles at me. Tears stream down my face when I swipe to send him to voice-mail, then text Sadie.

Me: Can I stay at your place tonight?

The phone rings again almost instantly with a call from her. "Ayda? What's going on? Are you okay?"

"Yeah...I just can't go home tonight. Do you mind if I stay with you?"

"Of course, you can stay with me. What happened? Did Dare do something? I'll tear him a new one, you know I will."

Sadie can always make me laugh through my tears. "No, but I don't want to see him right now. It's a long story."

"Well, I have wine and ice cream. Get your ass over here and tell me."

"On my way. Thanks, Sade."

When I arrive, Sadie takes one look at my tear streaked face and yanks me into her house. "I'll kill him," she says, assuming it's Dare who has me so upset. I argued with myself all the way over whether to tell her or not, but I know Sadie. She's a hardass and she isn't going to let me take any shit. She'll go right to the cops, and then Dare.

"It's not him...well, not really," I mumble.

"Ayda, you have bruises on your neck that look a hell of a lot like fingers and your lip is busted. Are you telling me you did that to yourself?" she demands, leading me to the couch.

Sobs rack my body while Dare rings my phone for the tenth time. I have to tell her. I need to tell someone.

The whole story pours out. The only thing I leave out is ISH and Dare's cyber-stalking. Sadie brings me an icepack for my lip and a glass of cold water to soothe my throat.

"We should get you checked at the hospital," she says.

"I'm okay. My throat is sore, but I can breathe. There's nothing they can do." I grab her hand. "And we can't call the police."

"Clearly," she sighs, and I look up at her in surprise. "I'm not naïve. I know how this shit works. This psycho is related to a senator who used to be a judge. There's no doubt he can make things go his way. Is there any security video of the fight?"

"No."

"So, it's his word against Dare's."

"A senator's son versus an ex-con," I agree.

"Fuck."

"Yeah."

Dare rings my phone again, and I can't take it anymore. Taking a deep breath, I hit accept.

"What the hell is going on, Ayda?" he demands before I can say hello.

"I'm spending the night with a friend."

"Something is wrong. I can hear it in your voice. What happened?"

"Nothing, I...need some time. I don't think we

should see each other for a while." The words are so hard to get out.

"What? What the fuck? What did I do?"

Tears threaten again, and I try to swallow the lump in my throat. "Nothing, you're perfect. I just need some time. Please, stop calling me. I have to go." I hang up before he can respond, and he instantly rings back. A text appears after I send the call to voicemail.

Dare: Talk to me, whatever is going on, we can figure it out.

Dare: Ayda, damn it.

A few minutes pass before his last message.

Dare: This isn't over.

But it is. It is over, and the sooner he accepts that, the safer he'll be.

———

"Make me a list of what you need," Sadie says while we sit at her kitchen table the next morning. "You can stay here as long as you want."

I'm grateful to have a friend like her. "Shit. My laptop is at his place."

"No problem. I can get it. I'll stop by after work."

I hand her a list of things to grab from my apartment. Maybe I'm being dramatic, but I can't bear to go back and listen to him next door. He'll never let up trying to talk to me through the walls like we used to, and I can't take it right now.

"I have to be at the studio this afternoon, but I'll be back around seven. I'll pick up dinner. Tacos?" I suggest.

"Sounds good. One of my patients today is a man who always thinks he knows more than I do, despite my degree. If he drives me too crazy, I may return with alcohol." She grins at me from the door. "See you tonight."

"Thanks for everything, Sadie."

"Anytime."

Silence fills the house, and I let myself cry for a few minutes. I'm trying to keep my shit together. I'm used to physical pain, but this is different. For the last few months, I've felt something I didn't even recognize until now. Hope. Emily Dickinson called hope *the thing with feathers*. I guess she's right, since it can up and fly the fuck away, leaving nothing but the memories of how it felt.

I was happy before. Well, content at least. I was satisfied with my solitary life, my dancing, and an occasional day out with Sadie. Then Dare came along and made me want things I thought I couldn't have. He gave me hope for a different future, with love and maybe even kids. Even with the pain of losing him and that future shredding my heart into tiny scraps, I wouldn't change a thing about the time I spent with him.

He changed me, gave me confidence to crawl out of my hole and face the world. No matter how badly I want to curl up and bemoan my fate, I won't let myself go back to that. I may have lost the most important thing in my life, but I still have a new job I love, and friends who care about me.

CHAPTER
THIRTEEN

DARE

Ayda broke up with me. One second her hand is on my cock, teasing me, and a few hours later, she needs some time away from me. I'm not buying it. Something is going on that she isn't telling me. I need to get to her, but I'm stuck in this stupid fucking apartment like a dog in a pound. Every fiber of me wants to say fuck it, and go after her, but I won't be able to help her if I'm locked up.

Landon, Justus, and Jeremy show up an hour after I call them, laptops in hand. "He must have gotten to her, threatened her," I tell them as they sit in my living room. I was worried she may have even been taken against her will, but her friend, Sadie, answered her phone last night after Ayda was asleep. She told me the same thing, to give her some time to think. It's not what I wanted to hear, but at least I know she's okay.

S.M. SHADE

Justus's fingers fly across the keyboard. "Talbot left the hospital yesterday, against medical advice. No hits on his credit card, but the senator just transferred a quarter of a million dollars to someone."

"A bribe?"

"Give me some time. I'll try to track the money."

I don't have time. I meet with my lawyers in a few days and I've made it clear I won't be pleading this down. I want to go to trial. I have a plan to bring both of those assholes down, but if it falls through, I could be going away for a long time.

"I've got Sadie's address," Jeremy says, smiling up from his computer. He texts it to my phone.

My gaze darts to the door. "No fucking way, man," Landon says, glaring at me. "If you leave, you'll be in jail by tonight. They'll hold you until trial and that could be months away."

"Fuck!" My hands run through my hair, and I feel the need to hit something. "I know! I can't sit here and do nothing!"

"Then get your ass online and find out who the senator's cronies are. He was a judge. I'm sure he has a few others in his pocket. You can bet he'll be calling in a favor for your trial. You messed up his son's pretty face."

He's right. I need to focus. I can't chase my girl and bring her back, but I can fight for my freedom so I don't lose her for good.

The guys spend a caffeine fueled night at my place, except for Landon who has to be home before dawn. The shit we manage to put together on the senator and his son is nothing short of devastating. They're going to be sorry they fucked with my woman.

Late in the afternoon, I hear Ayda's door slam, and I'm a second away from being out mine when Justus grabs me. "Your ankle, dude. You can't."

Fuck. Fuck. Fuck.

I don't have long to brood before Sadie knocks on my door. "Hey, Ayda left her laptop here and she needs it for work," she says, entering without waiting for an invitation.

"Where is she? Is she okay?" I demand, following her into my living room.

"She's hanging in there. Thinking some things through."

I've had it. "Cut the shit. I know something happened. She didn't change her mind in the two hours she was gone. Did Talbot contact her?"

Sadie gives me a look. She isn't going to tell me, but her expression says it all. "Fine. Since she won't talk to me, give her a message. I'm going to fix this. Whatever he did or said to scare her away from me is bullshit. Tell her I'll give her a couple of days, then I'm coming after her and this damn anklet isn't going to stop me."

Sadie suppresses a grin. "Maybe I was wrong about you."

"Were you wrong about me?" Justus asks, sidling up beside her with a smile.

"Never really gave you any thought." She dismisses him, which only eggs him on.

"You don't have to think about me, sweets. The fantasy could never be as good as the real thing. I'd be happy to come by tonight."

"Don't call me sweets. And I don't want stripper glitter all over my house. I'll pass."

A snort of laughter comes from Jeremy, and Justus steps back, feigning offense. "I don't wear glitter!" A smile stretches across his face. "Unless you're into that. I could pull it off. My buddy has a unicorn costume women seem to like. Sparkly unicorn turn you on? My horn is huge."

Sadie turns to me. "Is he serious?"

I shrug. "We're never sure."

"I'll give Ayda your message." She hesitates. "I'm worried about her. I know you're facing charges, but, do whatever you have to do to keep her safe. She's had more than enough pain in her life."

"I'm on it," I swear, walking her to the door.

"That chick wants me so bad," Justus claims after she leaves.

Jeremy leans back and cracks his knuckles. "Yeah, I could tell by the way she was completely repulsed by you."

"You don't know women. She's playing hard to get."

"I don't think she's playing."

"Either way." He shrugs and sits back down with his computer. A few seconds later, he shouts, "Got him! Dare! We got that motherfucker. Look at this."

"The quarter mil payment went to a Judge Powers. There was also a deposit sent to Sarah Noort. She's a court clerk in charge of assigning cases. I'd bet my left ball he paid her to make sure your assault case lands in Power's court, then bribed Powers to throw the book at you."

I'm on the phone with Mason in a matter of seconds. "We need to meet with the lawyer. I have evidence that I'm being set up."

"It better be good because the prosecutor just upped the charges to aggravated assault with a deadly weapon."

"I didn't have a weapon," I growl, gritting my teeth.

"Then we need to look into the prosecutor too."

CHAPTER
FOURTEEN

AYDA

It's been almost a week without Dare, and every day has been longer than the last. I drag myself out of bed, work on whatever project needs done that day—usually a book cover or two—then head to the studio. Lisa offered me a full time position teaching her beginner class. After thinking about it for a couple of days, I accepted.

I need something to keep my mind occupied, and the only time I don't feel like someone is slowly turning me inside out is when I'm lost in the beauty of dance. It's my escape. Watching a class full of smiling, giggling elementary school kids fall in love with ballet the way I did is the high point of my day. The hours I spend dancing alone after the last class help me stay centered and keep me from brooding on what I lost.

Sadie has been great, but I can't impose on her anymore. It's time to go home. I have to get back to my life. I've decided that moving would be the easiest choice. There are plenty of apartments available that don't share a wall with the man I love, but can't have.

Dare has stopped trying to get in touch with me. After a week of sending his calls to voicemail and not answering his texts, he must've figured out I'm not going to change my mind. No matter how much I want to.

After my two afternoon classes are over, I pack up my stuff and start home. At least I don't have to worry about running into Dare, since he still can't leave his apartment. He recently met with the lawyer and prosecutor to reject a plea deal. He's going to trial. I know this because Justus and Sadie have been texting back and forth all week. She says she's not interested, that she's just screwing with him, but that didn't stop her from showing me the most horrible picture of him in nothing but a unicorn horn and body paint.

I make my way to my door as quietly as possible, hoping Dare won't open his and see me. It's going to be hard enough being able to hear him again. Thankfully, my lease is up in less than eight weeks, and I can start looking for a new place. I breathe a sigh of relief when I close my door behind me.

I'm busy chucking all of the rotten food out of my fridge when I hear my door close again. I knew Sadie would follow me.

Suddenly, I'm looking at the floor. "Sorry about this, tiny dancer, but Dare will never quit pestering me if I don't bring you to him. He's a bitch like that."

"Put me down, Justus!" I screech, bobbing over his shoulder while he carries me through the apartment and out the front door. "I don't want to see him! I can't!"

No! What if Talbot is watching? He said if I stayed away, he wouldn't show up in court, the case would get dismissed, and Dare would be okay. They're about to fuck everything up.

Justus ignores my pleas and threats and carries me into Dare's apartment. He holds my arm a moment to steady me once I'm placed back on my feet, face to face with Dare. Dare gives him a terse nod, and he sighs. "I know when I'm not wanted."

The front door closes behind him, leaving me alone with a seriously pissed off man. His gaze singes my skin as it travels from my feet to my face, settling on my eyes. There are a million things I want to say, but I can't seem to get my mouth to work.

"Ayda," he mumbles, then I'm in his arms, being kissed within an inch of my sanity.

I should leave. I should run far and fast for his own good, but my body doesn't give a shit about what I think. It softens and molds to him, reveling in every stolen kiss and caress.

"Fuck, I missed you," Dare says, pulling me tighter to him.

"I missed you, too." My fingers run through his hair. "But I can't be here."

His forehead touches mine and his breath wafts across my face. "I love you, Ayda. Stop running from me."

My heart swells until it shatters. He finally said the words I wanted to hear so badly, but it doesn't matter. We still can't be together. "I love you, too, but..."

"No. No buts." He leads me to the couch and pulls me down with him. "Tell me the truth. What happened?

I know Talbot or his father is behind this. I'm trying to handle things, but I can't fix it if I don't know what's going on."

"Wait until after your trial," I plead. "It's only a few weeks away. Then maybe we can see each other again. I have to go."

"Ayda, damn it!" He grabs my arm when I try to rise. "Tell me! I'm going out of my mind here."

I'm exhausted, mentally and physically from the constant stress. Watching behind me every minute, wondering if he's there. If he is, it's probably already too late.

As if he heard my worst fears, my cell dings with a text message.

Unknown: Have it your way, bitch. He's never getting out. And your day is coming.

The expression on my face alerts Dare, and I give up, handing him my phone.

His face hardens, his cheeks going a deep scarlet. "He's threatening you?" The anger in his voice scares me. "Which one is it? The senator?"

There's no point in keeping anything from him anymore. Tears overflow as I reply, "First, promise no matter what I tell you, you won't leave this apartment. I've screwed up your life enough. Don't get sent to jail for breaking your house arrest."

He fights to control his anger, swallowing it down. His voice is softer when he speaks again. "I won't leave." His hands grip my arms, making me face him. "Tell me."

"Talbot. He said if I stayed away from you, he

wouldn't show up in court and the case would get dismissed. You wouldn't go back to prison. And if I didn't, he'd get his father to make sure you got the maximum sentence."

I bury my face in his chest. "I didn't want to leave you. I love you. I wanted to protect you, but I couldn't, and now he's going to—."

"Shh." Dare pulls me into his lap. "He isn't going to do anything, Ayda. I told you. I've got this handled. You should've come to me."

"I don't want to lose you again."

His big palm is warm on the back of my head as he strokes my hair. "You won't lose me. I'm not letting you out of my sight."

"He's watching me." Dare's entire body stiffens beneath me. "He said he'd be watching me. And just now, he knew I was with you."

"Fuck. I'm taking care of this right now." I'm afraid he's going to break his promise and go barging out the door to look for Talbot, but he grabs his phone and dials. "Mason? Yeah, I've got a problem. No, I didn't leave the apartment! It's Talbot. He's stalking Ayda. Yeah, around the clock. She'll be staying with me. You can post him outside. Got it, thanks, man."

"Mason has a security staff. Someone will be with you at all times until this is over." He pins me with a solemn gaze. "All times, Ayda. If you go to the dance school, the grocery store, wherever, he goes with you, understand?"

Exhausted, I nod, and curl up beside him.

"Everything will be okay, babe. You just have to trust me."

I feel like a child being escorted around by a bodyguard, but it can't be helped. I'm always accompanied by either Alex, who it turns out is Mason's brother, or Devon, one of his security staff. One of them is always outside Dare's apartment when I'm there, and they drive me to work at the dance studio, making sure no one unfamiliar approaches me.

Dare tries to convince me to take a break from teaching until this whole thing is over, but I refuse. I've just started teaching and I don't want to let Lisa down. Plus, I'd go crazy being trapped at home all the time, watching Dare climb the walls.

Alex walks me into the studio, then takes a seat in the lobby while I teach. A new girl is starting today, a seven-year-old with autism, and her mother brings her a bit early so we can help her feel comfortable in the new surroundings.

"Hi, you must be Ms. Light," I say, walking to meet them. "I'm Ayda."

"Please, call me Cara. And this is Ginny." She smiles down at a tiny blond girl, who's glancing around the room, taking it in.

She looks at me when I kneel down to her level. "Hi, Ginny! Look at your pretty tutu! I'll bet purple is your favorite color."

She responds with the most adorable gap toothed smile I've ever seen. Her mother has explained that she's nonverbal but understands everything that's being said to her. A few of the other kids filter in and start chasing each other around the room. Ginny eyes them, warily.

"Daisy!" I call to one of my other students, a sweet girl a few years older than Ginny, and she rushes over, ponytail bobbing. I introduce the two of them. "Ginny is starting today and she's a little nervous. Will you be her buddy and help her follow along?"

"Sure!" Ginny's mom quickly explains that she doesn't talk, but Daisy isn't fazed. That's the best thing about children, the way they accept everyone. A few asked about the scar on my face when I started teaching, but it was just curiosity, not fear or repulsion. Ginny takes Daisy's hand and lets her lead her to the barre.

Cara lets out a little sigh of relief, and I turn to her. "She'll be fine."

And she is. Cara stays to watch in case Ginny needs something. She communicates using sign language, and I remind myself to find a program online to learn it. If she continues with dance, I want her to be able to speak to me. The class goes well, and everyone leaves happy. My heart swells at the sight of Ginny laughing and giggling on her way out. I hope ballet will give her another way to express herself.

I'm cooling off, drinking a bottle of water when Betty, the woman who works the desk part time, sticks her head through the door. "Someone here to see you, Ayda."

I'm instantly alarmed. "Who?"

"I didn't get her name."

Her. What a relief. I shouldn't worry. After all, Alex is standing guard outside. "I'm coming." It's probably one of the mothers asking about a private lesson.

Thankfully, Betty and Alex are the only other people present in the lobby for the next few minutes. Still dressed in my leotard and ballet shoes, I round the corner and come face to face with Victoria. She's dressed in dance clothes, her hair in a pile on her head. A taunting smile widens her face.

"What the fuck are you doing here?" I demand.

Her eyes flash with anger. She expected me to be afraid, but all I can feel is rage. I've never done anything to this woman, other than dance better than her, and she ruined my life.

"Now, what kind of greeting is that for a prospective teacher? I heard this school was looking for an instructor for a beginner class. I figure I can fit it in between my competitions."

She's here to screw with my head, to remind me how everything hangs in the balance, and with one shove, her boyfriend can bring it crashing down. Something comes over me. I don't know if I'd call it rage, because I still feel calm, eerily calm.

I feel calm when I slam my fist into her mouth, when I grab her hair and jerk her head back so I can land the next punch on her nose, which sprays blood onto my clothes. My voice is level when I shove her to her knees and say, "You're going to walk out of here and never come near me again, do you hear me? Tell your psycho boyfriend I'm done fucking with both of you."

Bawling and holding her nose, she nods frantically. It's not good enough.

"Answer me!"

Hateful eyes glare up at me. "It's your fault he doesn't want me! He spends all his time following you!"

This bitch is crazy. "Because you told him to!"

"No! I don't give a shit what you do."

"But you came here."

"I thought he'd be here," she whispers.

Letting her go, I leave her with a warning. "Let this be the end of it, Vicky. If you show up again, this isn't going to end well for you or him. I have nothing left to lose. You don't want to fuck with me."

Alex grabs her arm when she gets to her feet and escorts her outside. He has a big grin on his face when he returns. "Damn, girl. That was brutal."

"She deserved it."

He holds up his palms. "Not saying she didn't. I'm sorry I didn't stop her."

"You're supposed to keep Talbot and the senator away from me, not a woman dressed as a dancer. She knew what she was doing."

Lights flash across the front of the school, and two officers enter. Shit. I've never been in trouble in my life. Alex knows one of them and intervenes, dragging him aside where they talk in low murmurs. They approach me and the look on Alex's face tells me I'm not going to like what I hear.

"The bitch is pressing charges, Ayda. You have to go with them, but I swear, I'll have you out in a few hours."

With a sigh, I glance from one of the officers to the other. "I have an order of protection against her and her boyfriend. Does that make a difference?"

"Yes, we can arrest her, and she'll face charges for breaking the order, but that doesn't mean you won't have to answer for assaulting her. Be sure your lawyer knows about the protective order, and that you were defending yourself."

The officer is reluctant to arrest me, since they can see

what's going on, but their hands are tied. "Do you have to cuff her?" Alex asks, when one of the officers produces a set of handcuffs.

"It's protocol. We can take it outside, though." So far, no one but Betty has been witness to all this, and I'd rather the few students and parents present not see me get arrested.

My heart speeds up as I'm read my rights, my hands are cuffed in front of me, and I'm put in the back of a cop car. I'm scared, but I'm trying not to let it get the best of me. I've heard the horrible stories about the things that happen in jail. Never imagined I'd get to see firsthand.

"Just a few hours, Ayda," Alex swears. "Everything will be okay."

Forcing a smile, I nod. "Don't let Dare find out. He'll leave the apartment." Alex agrees, then goes back to talking to one of the officers while I'm driven away.

It's pretty much what I expect. I'm taken to a room, fingerprinted and photographed before being put into a small cell with three other women who obviously aren't having the best day either. I get a few odd looks, considering I'm still in a leotard, but they're too lost in their own misery to comment.

A long, cement bench stretches along one wall, and I curl up in the corner of it, trying to get warm. It's so cold in here, I'm surprised I can't see my breath. A toilet sits in the corner, with a waist high wall separating it from the rest of the cell. I've never been so glad to have a strong bladder, because there's no way I'm pissing in public.

My teeth chatter, and I tuck my arms around my knees. I can't believe I'm here. No matter how hard I try to move on, Vicky and Talbot aren't going to let me. They're never going to stop fucking with my life. Now, I'll have a criminal record. I allow myself a few minutes to wallow in self-pity before the sight of Vicky's face flashes in front of me. Her shocked expression when I hit her was almost funny. Through the fear and cold, I feel another emotion—satisfaction.

I didn't take her shit. Breaking her nose was totally worth a few hours in this concrete sewer. Leaning my head back against the wall, I let myself get lost in a daydream of Dare and I alone on an island with no threats hanging over our heads. His hard, tatted body laid out in the sun. His arms around me, dragging me into the surf while I laugh and struggle against being tossed into the water. Peace with the man I love. That's all I want. It's not that much to ask for, is it?

"Ayda Brooks." I jerk back to reality when an officer calls my name. He leads me out to the room where I was fingerprinted then hands me my coat and phone.

"What's happening?"

"You're being released on your own recognizance. Sign this and be sure to show up for your court date."

My hands shake as I sign the paperwork. The officer leads me through a door to the lobby where Alex rushes to meet me. "Are you okay?"

"Y-yeah," I stammer, relieved but overwhelmed.

His lips press together, and he gives me a warm hug. "I'm sorry, hun. I shouldn't have let this happen. Let's get you home."

Alex cranks up the heat in his car and drives me home. Well, back to Dare's apartment. I've barely been home since we got back together. A lot of my clothes and toiletries have migrated next door.

I'm barely inside when Dare rushes up to me. "What the hell happened? Is that your blood?" he demands, taking in my stained clothes.

"She's fine." Alex speaks up before I can. "Victoria showed up at the studio, trying to start shit, but your girl here handled it."

Heavy palms fall on my shoulders while he looks me in the eye. "Ayda, are you hurt?"

"No, well, my knuckles are a bit sore." Alex chuckles and heads to the kitchen.

"What happened?"

"Like Alex said, she showed up and asked for me. Anyway, I lost my temper and kind of...hit her in the mouth."

Dare's lips curl up. "Kind of hit her in the mouth?"

"And the nose. That's where the blood came from." Wincing, I close and open my fist. "I didn't think it would hurt that bad to hit someone. I've never done it before."

Dare laughs, shaking his head. If I didn't know better, I'd say it's pride I see in his eyes. Alex returns and hands Dare an ice pack.

"Before you tear Alex a new one, she was dressed as a dancer. He had no reason to see her as a threat. And he got me out of jail as fast as possible."

Dare whips around so fast it's a wonder the breeze doesn't knock me over. His jaw hardens, and he glares at Alex. "She was in fucking jail? Why the hell didn't you call me?"

"Because she asked me not to and she was right. You

would've been out the door and we'd have even more problems to deal with. She's out and safe. The charges will be dropped once the judge sees the protective order."

"She's my fucking woman! You don't keep that shit from me!"

I turn to Alex, giving him a quick hug. "Thanks for getting me out of there. You should go."

"I'll be right outside," Alex replies, fighting a grin.

Dare jerks me into his arms. "God, Ayda. Jail is not a place for someone like you."

"Someone like me?" I mumble into his shirt.

"You're too tiny, too sweet to be surrounded by animals in a cell."

"There were a few other women. They didn't bother me. I felt sorry for them. I'm fine."

My phone buzzes in my pocket. "It's Lisa. I have to talk to her. If she fires me, I won't be surprised."

"You aren't going back to work until this is over, Ayda," Dare says.

"You can't tell me where I can go."

"The fuck I can't. If I have to keep you tied to the bed, I'm keeping you safe."

Turning my back, I answer the call. Lisa is extremely supportive about everything and doesn't blame me, but when I mention not coming in until everything blows over, she agrees it's probably best for everyone involved. "You always have a job here, Ayda. I want you to come back," she assures me.

Dare stares at me when I hang up, looking satisfied that he got his way. In a huff, I stalk away from him and into the bedroom to grab some clothes. Between the blood on me and the hours spent a few feet from a toilet, I've never felt so disgusting.

He leans on the door jamb and watches me silently, his arms crossed across his chest, making his biceps bulge. His gray sweat pants hang low, showing the V of muscle my tongue always finds its way to. For some reason, the sight of him—or maybe it's more my reaction to the sight of him—pisses me off.

If he thinks he can start telling me where to go or what to do, he's lost his mind. Sending Justus to carry me over here, telling me I'm not going to work, he obviously thinks he can make me do whatever he wants.

"What are you doing?" he asks, when I push past him.

"Taking a bath, or do you think I need your permission for that, too?" I'm taking out my shitty day on the wrong person, but I can't stop myself. It doesn't help that he seems to find my little tantrum amusing. "I'm running next door to get some panties. I'll be right back. There's no need to send one of your goons after me again."

Alex steps out of his car when he sees me come out, but I wave him away, holding up a finger to show him I'll just be a second. It's not the same finger I'm tempted to show Dare. I grab a few pair of underwear and my comfy sweats before marching back to Dare's apartment.

I'm smacked in the face by citrus scented steam when I enter the bathroom where Dare is turning off the faucet. "You ran me a bath?" I ask, stunned.

CHAPTER
FIFTEEN

DARE

Ayda was so fucking adorable storming around the apartment. It was everything I could do not to laugh. She's a pent up ball of anger and frustration right now, and I know how she feels. I've been there.

Her scowl dissolves when she returns and sees the tub full of warm water, the lights turned low. "You ran me a bath?"

"Yes." She stares at me like I'm trying to trick her when I approach and kneel down, removing her ballet shoes. Judging by how raggedy they are, I don't think they're meant to be worn out of the studio, much less to jail and across slushy, snowy streets. I peel off her clothes until she's standing in front of me, nude. "You had a bad day."

Her eyes well up, and she nods. Holding my hand, she steps into the tub, then sinks back into the hot water with a grateful moan. A giggle escapes her when she peeks up at me.

"What's so funny?"

"I was going to suggest you get in with me, but..." She shrugs.

"I can't fit in this tub by myself. It's probably a good thing. You need to relax, and if I was in there with your wet, slippery body against mine, you wouldn't get much rest."

"Sex fiend," she teases.

"Only since you came along." Makeup streaks her face and neck, so I grab her little puffy sponge thing—I don't know what the hell it's called—and lather it up with body wash. She closes her eyes, leaning her head back as I stroke it across her throat. As the makeup dissolves, pale green and yellow skin is visible beneath.

"What the fuck?"

Her eyes fly open. "Oh! I forgot."

"You forgot you had massive bruises on your neck?" She sits up, wrapping her arms around her knees, and I try to tamp down my anger. I don't want to scare her, but if these are from Talbot's visit to her, they must've been severe for it to still be visible. No wonder she locks the door when she showers. I didn't mention it because I thought she was still nervous and needed to feel safe.

"Talbot?" I ask, trying not to grit my teeth.

She nods and lays her head on her knee.

"I thought he just threatened you. You never said he touched you."

"I didn't want you to go after him and screw up your house arrest."

I rest my palm on her cheek, and she nuzzles it. "Did

he...sexually assault you?" If she says yes, she's signing that fucker's death warrant right here and now.

"No, he choked me, slapped me once. That's all." Her whole body is tense again.

That's all. I need him in front of me now. I need to break him in half. "Okay." It's a struggle to keep my voice even. "We don't have to talk about it right now." She needs to take it easy.

A comfortable silence falls between us while I wash away the remnants of her terrible day. "Relax a while, babe, and I'll order us some dinner. What sounds good?"

"Something greasy, then something drowning in sugar."

"You got it."

He hurt her, *choked* her. I shouldn't be surprised since her skin is proof of what he's capable of, but all I can think of now is squeezing his throat the way he did hers, watching his eyes bug out, watching him panic.

Watching him die.

Landon picks up on the first ring, and I step out on the balcony, explaining everything to him.

"We can't," Landon says.

"What?"

"We can't feed him to the pigs. Dare, think, man. He has a case against you and his girlfriend has a case against Ayda. You two will be the top suspects if he goes missing. I know it's hard, but you have to wait. Let this play out the way we planned. Then, if you feel the same, I'm sure he could have an accident in prison."

He's right, damn it.

"Do I need to come over there and keep you from doing something stupid?"

"No. Ayda's here. I just…"

"I know. If it were Zoe, I'd feel the same way. It's hard to just sit tight, I know. I've done my share, but you need to let us handle this. We've got your back and Ayda's. Go be with the only girl who doesn't see what an asshole you are."

Through the balcony door, I watch Ayda emerge from the bathroom, dressed in sweats with her hair falling around her shoulders. "All right, I have to go."

"Later, man."

My heartbeat has slowed, and I'm not quite as worked up after venting to Landon, but I still have every intention of seeing Talbot six feet under. After making a quick call to a local restaurant, I join Ayda on the couch.

"Walking Dead or Game of Thrones?" she asks.

"Your choice." She snuggles into my arms, smelling of citrus and the cucumber lotion she uses. Her upper body rests on my chest while her shapely legs tangle with mine. There's an ache in my chest I don't recognize, but I know it has to do with this beautiful woman with the smart mouth who has completely changed the way I see my future. She makes me want good things, to be the type of man she deserves. Beside that ache in my chest is another feeling I barely remember. Hope.

If I wasn't already sure Senator Coulter was pulling strings, the fact that my trial date is set for only three weeks from now would be proof. It typically takes months to go to trial. Three weeks until I can set things right. Until then, I plan to keep her right here with me. Safe in my arms. In my bed.

Being cooped up isn't nearly as bad with Ayda by my side, but I know it's starting to wear on her. Other than an occasional trip for groceries and other necessities, she hasn't left the apartment in almost two weeks.

She met with a lawyer last week and agreed to drop the charges against Victoria if she'd do the same. At least she's not in trouble and won't end up with a criminal record. Unfortunately, that means Victoria gets away clean once again.

Valentine's Day is coming up, and I don't know what to do for her, since I can't leave the house. It's time to call in reinforcements.

My sister, Leah, answers her phone and listens when I explain what I want to do. "I'd love to!" she exclaims. "I can't wait to meet her! And I love the spa!"

"Then get your ass here by nine a.m. kid."

She hangs up with a squeal that makes me smile. The girl is pure energy. My next call is to Landon, who gives me a ton of shit before putting his wife on the phone. "Zoe, I need help."

She listens to me explain, then promises to be over by ten on Valentine's morning.

When Valentine's Day comes, Ayda groans, "Why do I have to be out of bed so early?"

"Because I have a surprise for you." She jumps when I smack her ass. "Now get ready. My sister will be here soon."

Her eyes pop open. "Your sister's coming?"

"She's on her way."

With a smile, Ayda hops out of bed and heads for the shower. She's excited to meet the only family I have left. Since my mom failed to protect Leah, and still denies

Dad's brother molested her, we've cut her out of our lives. After seeing what Ayda has to deal with when it comes to her mother, I'm grateful to have at least one stable family member.

Leah bounces through the door in a cloud of enthusiasm and smiles. My kid sister has always been the happy, outgoing one who can make anyone smile. Ayda's going to love her. She gives me a big hug, then asks, "Okay, where is she?"

Ayda enters the room, and Leah bounds over to her. "Hi! Dare told me he found a woman willing to put up with him, but I didn't believe it! And look how gorgeous you are, I'm totally jealous. We're going to have so much fun today!"

Ayda laughs and hugs her, raising her eyebrows at me. "Ayda, this is Leah. I've arranged for you two to go to a spa for the day. Alex will accompany you. According to him, he's man enough to get a pedicure."

"It's going to be great. We'll get our nails and hair done, get a massage, relax in the steam room. Oh! And they have this cute restaurant that makes the best little cakes you've ever tasted," Leah gushes.

"Sounds great," Ayda replies. "I'm dying to get out of here for a while."

Alex taps on the door before entering. "Ready to be pampered, ladies?"

The excited expression on Ayda's face makes my day when she turns to hug me. "Happy Valentine's Day, baby. Go have fun."

"I love you," she murmurs.

Leah's stare bores holes into my skull, a hopeful smile on her face until I reply. "I love you, too."

"Your masseuse better be female!" I call out as they leave, grinning when Ayda and Leah giggle.

They won't be back until this evening, which gives me plenty of time to prepare for our date night. I can't take her out, but I'm going to do my best right here. Zoe shows up right on time, accompanied by her best friend, Frannie.

"Okay, show me what you picked out," Zoe says once she and Frannie take a seat at the kitchen table.

There's a slight frown on Zoe's face when she sees the silver hummingbird necklace with a tiny diamond for an eye. "It's pretty and all, but I'm not sure it's her."

"It is. It reminds me of her."

"And you're making dinner tonight?"

"I'm having the Italian place deliver, but I need some stuff, you know, a box of chocolates, some flowers and candles."

Zoe gives me a look like I'm a puppy that tripped over its ears.

"Stop it."

"Sorry, but sometimes I let the fact that you're this big scary behemoth covered in tats make me forget you're really a sweetheart."

"No, I'm not," I growl.

Zoe grins at her friend. "Second opinion?"

"Fucking adorable," Frannie agrees, laughing.

Ugh. I hope Ayda likes what I have planned because I'm never going to live this down.

"Here's my card. Get whatever you think I need. The jewelry store knows you're coming for the necklace. They're holding it for me. Same thing goes at the lingerie store. Just give them my last name."

Zoe hops to her feet. "We'll take care of it. It's going to be so romantic! Landon better be planning something for me tonight or he's not getting laid for a long time."

Frannie laughs. "You know he is."

"Thanks, Zo," I tell her, and she gives me a wave on her way out the door.

Now, all I can do is wait.

Zoe and Frannie come in weighed down with shopping bags about an hour before Ayda is due back. "Damn, did you buy the whole store?" I exclaim, taking some of the bags.

"Just stand back and let us work, Bruiser," Frannie says, and Zoe cracks up.

"Bruiser. It's perfect."

"You girls are pushing it," I warn.

"Says the man who calls Landon *raisin*."

"Why raisin?" Frannie asks, tossing her fire red hair over her shoulder.

"Shrivels in the sun?" Zoe says, and Frannie turns to look at me, her mouth open.

I hold up my hands. "Justus came up with that one."

"Uh-huh." Zoe gives me a wave of dismissal. "Now, go away and let us work our magic."

God, how did I go from being a loner with a few guy friends to be surrounded by cocky women? They're turning our little group on its head. I can't imagine how things will be if Justus and Jeremy settle down. Someday, we're going to be outnumbered.

While they decorate the dining room, I call to order our dinner from Ayda's favorite Italian restaurant. By the time they leave, everything's ready. They've managed to turn my dining room into a romantic restaurant, complete with candles and flowers. A soft linen table-cloth covers the table, with two place settings arranged.

Zoe and Frannie both whistled with approval at the lingerie set I bought Ayda. Pale blue lace panties with a matching bra that leaves little to the imagination, with a matching lace robe which ends mid-thigh.

I tuck it inside the gift bag and add tissue paper on top. See, this is why I needed female help. I never would've bought a gift bag, tissue, or ribbons. I'd have handed it to her, or maybe laid it out on the bed. Fancy, frilly shit isn't something I understand, but for Ayda, I'll try anything.

The food delivery shows up just as Leah texts that they're fifteen minutes away, and it quickly gets shoved into the oven to keep it warm. I've showered, shaved, and I'm dressed in the only suit I own.

Fuck, I feel like an idiot standing in my living room all dressed up, waiting for her to come through the door. What the hell was I thinking? I don't do shit like this. Hell, the women I've been with were lucky to get a drink and cab fare home after. This woman has me by the balls, and worse, I have no desire to escape.

"Tell Dare I'll call him tomorrow," I hear Leah say as Ayda opens the door.

"I will. I had fun!" Ayda calls to her, stepping inside.

Her jaw drops at the sight of me standing there in a suit, holding a rose and feeling like a dumbass. Her bags get forgotten in the entryway. "What's going on?" she asks, a cautious smile on her face.

"I'm taking you on an official date."

Her forehead crumples. "You can't leave the house." She takes the rose and sniffs it, giving me a shy smile.

"We don't need to leave." I hold out my arm, and she giggles, taking it. "We have the best table in the place."

She allows me to lead her to the dining room, then freezes in the doorway, stunned. "You did all this?"

"I had some help." Spinning to face me, she leaps into my arms, and I catch her, backing her up against the wall. Her lips land on mine and her tongue wastes no time sliding in to rub and tease. Screw dinner. I just want to fuck her brains out, but I didn't do all this for nothing. "You smell amazing," I mumble, running my tongue over her collarbone.

"I was buffed, dipped and coated in every kind of cream and lotion imaginable." I set her down carefully and walk her to the table, pulling out her chair. "You made dinner?" she asks as I return from the kitchen with a tray bearing aluminum takeout containers.

"Something like that."

She giggles at the sight of them, then leans across the table to kiss my cheek. "This is the most romantic thing anyone has ever done for me."

"You deserve it."

"And you deserve what I have for you, but it'll have to wait until later. I'm starving." Her smile shifts something inside me. It always does. Seeing her happy feels like a weight has been lifted from my chest.

We spend the evening eating, talking, and laughing. For once, the shadow that's darkened our lives fades a little, letting us forget for a while that I have a court date less than a week away. When we finish, I pull a blue rectangular box from my pocket and place it in front of her.

"Dare, you've done enough. The spa, the dinner, you

didn't have to get me anything." Her soft hand slips into mine.

"It made me think of you," I confess when she holds the necklace in front of her face, watching the diamond catch the light.

"It's beautiful. A hummingbird?"

Coming around the table, I pluck it from her fingers and drape it around her neck. "Hummingbirds live on the edge of starvation and have to eat every fifteen minutes because their hearts beat so fast. They're tiny. And easy to mistake for weak creatures, but they're tough survivalists. Despite how hard it has to work to stay alive, it doesn't just live. It flourishes. Like you. After all you've been through, you keep fighting, keep trying to make things better for yourself and others. My hummingbird."

There are tears in her eyes when she gets to her feet, and I pull her into my arms. "I thought I was happy before," she sniffs. "I thought I was living, but I was just existing, going through the motions. Until your voice came through the wall and changed everything. You made me want more, with you, and out of life. I love you."

"I love you too."

Stepping back, she laughs and leads me to the bedroom where she finds the lingerie set in the gift bag on the bed. "Dare," she breathes, running her fingers over the material.

"That's more a present for me."

Her mischievous grin falls into place. "Not sure it'll fit you, but we can give it a shot."

Damn, I love her smart mouth.

CHAPTER
SIXTEEN

AYDA

I can't believe Dare went to so much trouble for Valentine's Day. The spa was wonderful, and I even decided on a Brazilian wax while I was there, something I don't usually do. Leah was a lot of fun, and she helped me shop for Dare's gift. I mean, what do you give a guy like him? So rough and mean when he needs to be, but soft hearted when it counts. I couldn't just get him a card or something too girly like a stuffed animal.

"I know just the thing," Leah announced and dragged me into a boutique. Alex stood guard outside the door while she held up a tiny scrap of material that can't possibly be considered panties. I ended up with them, though, along with a bra that barely covers my nipples, and sheer, thigh high stockings.

On our way out, I found a display of romantic knick-knacks and games, and impulsively bought a set of Love

Coupons. Each coupon offers a different sexy act, some innocent, some not so much. I can't wait for him to use them.

I'm tempted to wear the beautiful lingerie set Dare gave me, but I decide to stick to my original plan. "I have something for you, but I need a few minutes," I tell him, grabbing my bag and locking myself in the bathroom.

Standing in front of the mirror in tiny panties, a bra, and a white tutu, the stockings pulled up to mid-thigh, I almost chicken out. Every scar I have is on display. Maybe I'm making a fool of myself, trying to be sexy for him. Scars aren't sexy.

"Is everything okay?" he asks, tapping on the door.

Crap. How long have I been standing here staring at my body like something is going to change? Closing my eyes, I remember the loving way he kissed my scars, and take a deep breath. He's seen me naked. I'm being ridiculous.

"Fine," I call, then open the bathroom door, the Love Coupon booklet in my hand.

He freezes when I walk out, his eyes darkening with lust, and I know I have nothing to worry about. He looks like he wants to devour me, and I can't wait. "Fuck, Ayda, are you trying to kill me?"

Long strides tear across the hardwood floor until he's looking down at me. With the most innocent smile I can muster, I peek up through my lashes at him and open my hand holding the coupons. "Happy Valentine's Day."

"Love coupons, huh?" His grin turns wicked as he flips through the booklet and rips one out. Uh-oh. Maybe I should've read through them. He hands me one that says "Kinky card. Take me any way you please."

His gaze sweeps around the room, and he stalks over to the window, removing the cloth curtain tie-back before returning to me. His large hands travel over my ribs, cupping and massaging my breasts. "Hands out in front of you, baby."

Without a word, I hold them out, and he ties my wrists together. I gasp when I'm unexpectedly lifted off my feet. My arms loop around his neck, my tied hands resting on his nape while he carries me to the bedroom wall. I love the way he carries me around like I weigh almost nothing. Compared to his bulk, I guess I do.

"Keep those hands right there, babe," he orders. As much as I hate being told what to do in everyday life, I apparently don't have a problem with it in the bedroom. Without putting me down, he unhooks my bra and lets it fall to the floor, his mouth instantly covering my nipple. He's barely touched me and I'm already soaked for him, which he discovers when his hand slides between my legs, ripping the tiny panties away.

"Oh!" I cry out as his fingers plunge inside me.

"Yeah, you like that? I know you do." His low gravelly tone seems to vibrate through my whole body.

"You have no idea how many times I laid here and listened to you. Pictured you and what you were doing to yourself. I wanted to see the look on your face when you came. Right here," he says, burying himself inside me in one hard thrust that steals my breath. "I'm going to fuck you right here against the wall where you drove me fucking insane."

With my hands tied, all I can do is hold on and enjoy the ride. And damn, the man can fuck like a champ. After we try to buff most of the paint off of his wall, he turns and bends me over his bed. My arms are stretched in front of me, my feet dangling just above the floor when he slides back into me, gentler this time.

His hand runs up and down my legs. "I love these stockings. I'm going to buy you a hundred more."

His tongue travels up my spine until his hot breath fills my ear. "Look at you, bent over my bed, helpless, sexiest fucking thing I've ever seen."

I can't take it, the sound of his voice, the slow, devastating strokes, and the way he pauses to gyrate his hips, sending darts of pleasure shooting through me. "Dare," I plead.

"I know," he soothes. "You're so close. All you have to do is ask for it."

All pride goes out the window when he delivers another languorous stroke as if he could do this all night. "Please, make me come."

"Yeah?" he asks, leaning over me again. "Like this?"

The pad of his finger rubs one, two, three small circles on my clit, while he drives deep and fast. I can't believe the sound that comes from my throat. I've never screamed from an orgasm. I always thought it was exaggerated, something done in porn for the men's sake, but I was wrong. He pushes me over the edge, and I lose my fucking mind, screaming his name while I come harder than I ever have in my life.

When I regain my senses, his voice fills my ear. "I'm not done with you. Not even close."

The rest of the night is a sex soaked blur. I think he manages to take me on every surface in his apartment. It's nearly dawn when I beg for mercy, and we finally fall asleep.

My body aches, and I groan as I open my eyes the next morning. Dare's bright blues are staring at me, a satisfied grin on his face. "Ugh, what are you smiling about? I think you killed me."

"And you loved every second of it." His palm lands on my ass with a sharp crack. "Get up. Sadie called. Says she has some big news that she has to tell you in person."

"She's coming over?"

"On her way. I'll go make us some coffee." He drops a kiss on my forehead before rushing out of the room. His upbeat mood makes me smile. After weeks of moping around, all it took was a night of kinky sex to cheer him up. I'll have to keep that in mind.

Dare and I are sitting at the kitchen table, drinking coffee when Sadie shows up with a huge box of donuts. "Did you wipe out the bakery?" I laugh, and her face lights up.

"We're celebrating."

"Okay, what are we celebrating?"

"Karma," she announces, grabbing a cup of coffee and joining us. "You'll never guess who was assigned to me as a patient." She doesn't give us time to guess before announcing her news. "Victoria."

I pause with a donut halfway to my mouth. "Seriously?"

"Yep. She was performing the night before last and shattered her knee. It's bad. She'll walk again, but her dancing days are over."

Wow. Just like that. This woman ruined my life, put me in the hospital for months in the worst agony a person can feel. Then proceeded to rub it in every chance she got. I can't deny a part of me is thrilled to know she's lost the thing she loved most, the same way I did when dance was taken from me.

But it wasn't really taken from me. I'm not capable of performing professionally, but I can still dance, still teach and pass on my love of the art. I may have scars I have to live with, but more and more, I'm being shown that they don't matter nearly as much to others as I thought they did. I mean, I did manage to land the hottest man I've ever seen in person.

Dare tilts his head, catching my gaze. "Ayda? What's wrong? I thought you'd be happy."

"I am, but it seems wrong to revel in someone else's pain, no matter how much they deserve it."

"Don't tell me you feel sorry for that bitch!" Sadie exclaims.

"Not at all, but I can't, you know, celebrate it either."

Dare wraps his arm around my shoulders. "You are too damn good for me."

"Yeah, she is," Sadie agrees before I can argue with him.

"Sadie!"

"Sorry, he's right. You're too damn good-hearted. You make the rest of us look bad."

I shove her shoulder. "I am not, and I do not. Are you taking her as a patient?"

Sadie throws her head back, laughing, her blond ponytail swinging. "Hell no. I told my boss I have a conflict of interest. When he asked me what it was, I told him I hate her and there's a better chance I'd kick her in the knee than try to improve its function. He took me off of her case. Turns out it didn't matter anyway. Her insurance company dropped her because she hasn't paid the premiums, so she got kicked to the indigent hospital. Guess there isn't much money in dancing, huh?"

My eyes dart to Dare, who can't hide a grin. He shrugs. "Sometimes, people get what they deserve."

———

I don't know how Dare can be so calm when I'm a ball of nerves. This is it. The day we find out whether we're going to be torn apart for years. I expect the worst since I crossed Talbot, and he promised his father would make sure Dare gets the maximum sentence.

We haven't spent a day apart since the day I spent a few hours in jail, and I can't imagine my life without him now. I want him curled up on the couch with me every night while we argue over what TV shows to watch. I want his warm arms around me every night, protecting me from the world.

I need him.

It all comes down to today. Why is he so cool and calm when I'm about to sweat through my blouse?

"Everything's going to be fine. Trust me," Dare says, squeezing my hand after we park at the courthouse.

"I know. Tonight, when this is over, I'm going to give you the best blowjob you've ever had." My remark gets the response I was hoping for when he laughs and squeezes my hand again. I don't want him worrying about me or how I'll handle things when he should be worried for himself. He never talks about prison, but I know his time there affected him, and I can see the fear he tries to hide at the thought of going back.

"I'm holding you to that."

S.M. SHADE

We enter the courthouse, hand in hand, and I'm surprised to see a small crowd gathered outside the courtroom we've been assigned. I expected a couple of Dare's friends might show up, but everyone is here. Justus and Jeremy stand next to Landon, who wears an uncomfortable looking yellow suit that looks like it was borrowed from the Outbreak movie. A few feet away, Mason is deep in conversation with his brothers, Alex and Parker, their heads leaned together. Zoe and Leah sit on a bench, while Tucker leans on the wall beside them.

"I'm going to have a word with Mason," Dare says, and I nod, joining Zoe and Leah.

"How are you?" Leah asks, when I take a seat beside her.

"Trying not to throw up, how about you?"

"Same," she replies with a sigh. "Dare says he has it all under control, but I've been here before."

I give her a hug, and she wipes her eyes. My hands twist together while I fight to swallow the lump in my throat. I need to be strong if I don't want him worrying about me instead of his own future. Tucker places a hand on my shoulder. I haven't seen him since our sledding day, and the sight of him all cleaned up and healthy makes me smile. He's put on some weight—obviously all muscle—since his days living in the parking lot.

"Hey, Tucker. Thanks for coming," I tell him.

"Dare gave me a chance when I didn't think I deserved one. A job and a place to live. I've got his back." He squeezes my shoulder. "And he's not the only one. Look around, honey, he has a lot of support, and so do you. Everything will be okay."

"That's what everyone keeps telling me," I say with a reluctant laugh.

My hands tighten on the edge of the bench when another group approaches, stopping to talk just down the hall. Talbot is dressed in a sleek, clearly expensive suit, and I notice his jaw isn't wired anymore. His eyes meet mine, and he smirks, his expression that of a man who doesn't have a worry in the world.

It's the same expression his father is wearing as he nods at passersby. He's a senator, a former judge with powerful men at his beck and call, of course he has nothing to worry about. He's only here for appearances, to watch his son testify against the man who beat him. He was able to buy Talbot's way out of what should have been attempted murder charges for his attack on me. This should be a piece of cake.

The only one who doesn't look confident and pleased is Victoria. She's sitting in a wheelchair, her right leg encased in plaster from her thigh to her ankle. Her eyes find mine for a brief second before she looks away in misery.

The day I hit her, she told me that she had nothing to do with Talbot stalking me and trying to keep me away from Dare. Dare seems to think Talbot has some kind of obsession with me, too, but I know better. I was just an opportunity for him to be cruel. His girlfriend wanted me gone, and he was happy to inflict damage on another person. He's a psychopath, pure and simple.

Sadie comes rushing in. "Sorry I'm late. I had to shuffle some appointments around."

"You didn't have to come!" I cry, throwing my arms around my best friend.

She gives me a look like I may have been dropped on my head as a kid. "Of course I did!" Victoria catches her attention and she laughs, mumbling, "Karma is a bitch."

A man opens the doors to our courtroom a few minutes later to let everyone inside, but a commotion at the entrance draws our attention away. A group of suit clad men make their way down the hall toward us. Their clothes and demeanor scream Feds, but surely the FBI hasn't been brought in on an assault case. Oh god. Have they? Is this Talbot following through on his threat?

My gaze darts to Dare, who doesn't look surprised to see them. They walk right past him and make a beeline for Talbot's group. Confused, I start toward Dare.

Tucker's arm clamps onto mine, and I'm pulled to the ground. "Gun!" he shouts, grabbing Zoe's shoulder and shoving her to the floor, too.

The next few seconds seem to move in slow motion, like I'm watching it all unfold underwater. Talbot gets shoved against a wall. His hands are cuffed behind him by two agents while three more surround the senator who points a gun straight at Dare. People scream and flood out of the exits as security tries to get a handle on the situation, eventually locking down the building.

Sadie is tucked in a corner, filming everything with her phone. "Put the gun down, senator," an agent demands.

Montgomery ignores him. All his rage is focused on the man I love. "You! You did this! I'm being framed."

Dare laughs. Standing there with a gun pointed at him, he laughs, and I feel like I'm going insane. None of this can actually be happening. "Framed would mean you're innocent, when we both know you're guilty as hell, and so is your son. But I'm happy to accept the blame for calling attention to it. Don't worry, there are plenty of press out front waiting to see you in cuffs. I know how much you like being on TV."

He's goading him, daring him to shoot. "Shut up!" one of the agents barks at Dare while another inches closer to Montgomery. "This is your last warning. Drop the gun, or I will shoot you!"

Montgomery looks at the agent like he's dirt beneath his shoe, completely inconsequential. "Do you know who I am? You can't hurt me."

He raises the gun another fraction, and the agent proves him wrong. I've never actually heard a gunshot close-up before. It's deafening in the confined space. At first, I think it made a weird echo, until I see Dare's hand slam over his cheek, blood leaking through his fingers. Shouts fill the air, but I barely hear them over the buzzing in my ears. It's chaos as the agents struggle to get control of the situation, but all I can see is Dare.

Someone shouts my name, but I ignore it. He's shot. Dare's shot.

Finally, I reach him, and when he spins around, there's a small grin on his face. My mind can't seem to process what's going on. "He shot you," I whisper.

Dare removes his hand and swipes his cheek with his jacket sleeve. "It grazed me. I'm okay."

My knees buckle in relief, and he catches me, pulling me into his embrace. "It's okay. We're both okay, babe. It's over. I promise it's over."

"I don't understand what's happening. The FBI?" I squeeze him tighter, and he whispers in my ear.

"I told you not to worry. I had it all under control."

"Well, you got shot, so your control sucks," I reply. I'm still shaking from the adrenaline.

He chuckles while I survey the grisly scene in front of me. Senator Montgomery's body lies face down on the floor while the agents search him. Too little, too late. I guess being a senator was enough to get him through security without having to go through the metal detector.

Talbot is ranting and raving that everyone is going to pay. Sadie rushes over and hugs me. "Never a dull moment with you in my life," she says, her voice shaky. "Do you know what happened? Why they wanted him?"

"Multiple crimes," Dare explains. "Accepting bribes, bribing other judges—including the one who would've presided over my case today—embezzlement of campaign funds. Plus, he had child porn on his computer. That's why I didn't fight going to trial. We gave him the rope to hang himself with, and sure enough, he sprang into action to make sure I was convicted.

"Talbot is just as culpable. They'll both be going down for a long time. All the cases Montgomery presided over as a judge, and all the cases presided over by the judges he bribed will be re-examined." His hand threads into my hair, and he looks into my eyes. "Including yours."

"And your assault case?"

Dare's lawyer speaks up. "The state will likely drop the case now that the plaintiff is not a credible witness. They have plenty of evidence for his prior crime against you and for the stalking. Derek was acting in your defense."

Relief floods through me. Dare isn't going to prison. "It's really over?"

"Yes, it's really over." His blue eyes sparkle with happiness.

"Did you know this was going to happen today?"

"I hoped. The FBI wanted to wait until they could catch all the players off guard. The senator, Talbot, the judge set to preside over my trial, a prosecutor, even the court clerk who handed the judge the case, along with a few others who did his bidding." He gestures to the line of people now cuffed and seated along one wall.

"Why didn't you tell me?"

"I couldn't. It had to be kept close in case something went wrong, and I didn't want to get your hopes up."

I'm overwhelmed by all the sudden revelations. "Can we go home now?"

"The agents will probably want a word or two before they let anyone leave. Give me a second." He walks over to talk with one of the suited men.

We spend the next hour sitting in an empty courtroom while agents take our statements one by one. It seems silly to me since they were there and saw everything, but I guess when a standoff ends in death, it's protocol.

They finally let us go, and Dare grins, grabbing my hand. "Come on, you don't want to miss this." Just ahead of us, Talbot is being lead out in cuffs. As soon as they step out the door, he's surrounded with reporters screaming questions.

"Is it true your father paid off judges to keep you out of jail?"

"How many women have you assaulted?"

"Did you throw acid in a woman's face?"

Dare keeps us inside the doors where we can't be seen. "We don't have to go out that way. I just wanted you to see. People care, Ayda. They care what he did to you and the other women in his past. He won't get away with it anymore."

My heart thumps in my chest. I've hidden for so long, ashamed of what had been done to me, when it was never my fault. I'm done hiding.

"Let's go," I whisper, grabbing his hand.

A reporter takes one glance at my face and rushes over, quickly followed by three more. "Are you Ayda Brooks?"

Taking a deep breath, I face her camera. "Yes."

They all begin yelling over one another, and Dare intervenes, placing his large body in front of mine. "Ayda will answer a few questions. One at a time." His commanding voice and stature says he won't stand for any bullshit.

"Did Talbot Montgomery attack you with acid six years ago?"

"Yes, he did."

"Is that what caused the scarring on your face?" another woman speaks up, and Dare glares at her.

Laying my hand on his arm, I tell him, "It's all right."

"Yes, he threw acid on me at the request of his girl-friend, a fellow ballerina who wanted my scholarship. Thanks to his father, he got away with it, as did the dancer."

"Will you tell us the dancer's name?" another reporter asks.

The sight of Victoria in that wheelchair flashes before

me, now all alone and destitute, removed from the dance world forever, and likely facing charges of her own. "Not today. I'm sure that will come out soon enough."

They begin clambering again, talking over one another, so I hold up my hand. "I'm not the only woman victimized by Talbot Coulter. I don't want to go on about what happened to me. I've healed and I'm very happy with my life. I do want to encourage any of the other women he's hurt to come forward, to make sure he never gets out of prison and never has the chance to hurt anyone again."

I refuse to answer any more questions, and we rush to the car. I've never been so thankful for silence. The last few hours keep playing on a loop in my head. None of it seems real. Dare takes my hand, grounding me, and I smile at him. His love is a calm place in the middle of a storm.

"Let's go home."

EPILOGUE

DARE

ONE MONTH LATER.

"We're almost there. Don't be so impatient."

Ayda fidgets in her seat. I swear this woman can't stand a few minutes of suspense. Okay, maybe it's more than a few minutes, since I texted her over an hour ago to get ready because I had a surprise for her.

Justus and Jeremy both warned me I'm moving too fast, that asking Ayda to move in with me would be a mistake, but Landon told me to go for it. It took falling in love with my own girl to realize how normal his seemingly erratic behavior was when he fell for Zoe. These women drive us out of our minds, but as I gaze at her, her dark curls blowing in the cool air, I know I wouldn't change a thing.

I park on a neat, tree lined street only a few blocks from the dance studio, and she takes my hand, looking around.

"Who lives here?" she asks when I lead her up the steps of a two story Craftsman style house.

"We do," I reply, nonchalantly, unlocking the front door.

I stride in, and look back at her as she stands in the doorway, her feet glued in place. "What…did you buy a house?"

"Rented, for now, but we have the option to buy." A flick of a switch illuminates the living room. She gazes around at the rich wood and exposed beams overhead.

"We," she mumbles, taking it all in before turning to me. "Did you maybe forget something?"

"I don't think so." My back rests against the wall while my arms cross my chest. "We can change the colors, of course, or lay carpet if you like."

Shaking her head, a small smile tilts her lips. "So, we're moving in together?"

"Yes."

"And when did you make this decision?"

"A few days after we met."

Her expression betrays how much she likes that answer. She walks over by the large fireplace and leans against the wall, mimicking my stance by crossing her arms. "Maybe I don't want to move in together. I'm trying to think back, but for the life of me, I don't remember being asked."

Joy shines in her eyes, and I know she's teasing. If I wasn't a hundred percent sure this is what she wants too, I wouldn't have rented the place. Stalking over to her, I drop a brief kiss on her lips, then walk around the corner, leaning on the other side of the wall that separates the living room from the foyer.

"Ayda?" I say, a little louder than usual, so my voice can penetrate the wood and plaster. "Would you like to move in with me? I found a great little house near your job that you'll love."

Her giggle makes me smile. She always makes me smile. "Hmm, I may have a few conditions."

"Name them, babe."

"One, you can't store the peanut butter in the fridge anymore. It's unnatural. Two, I get the right side of the bed, and three, you must pleasure me sexually every night."

Fuck, I love this woman.

"I agree to all but the last one. I'm going to have to pleasure you every night and every morning."

"I suppose I can live with that."

She steps around the corner and leaps into my arms. "I love the house, and I love you. When can we move in?"

"About that..."

Justus and Jeremy burst through the front door, carrying a couch while bickering. "Tilt it, asshole!"

"I am tilting!"

"No, the other way! Christ, are you always an idiot, or just when I'm around?" Justus exclaims.

Ayda turns to me when Landon and Zoe walk in, carrying lamps and bags. "I don't know whether to kick you in the nuts or just stand in awe of your confidence." Wrapping my arm around her shoulder, I lead her through the room, so she can see the rest of the place. "What if I had said no?"

"I'd have lost a security deposit and returned the furniture." I shrug. "We can take back whatever you don't like, and you can pick."

Her smile gets bigger on our tour through the kitchen, dining room, guest rooms, bathrooms, and the master bedroom. She lets out a squeal at the sight of the large Jacuzzi tub in the master bathroom.

"I have one more room to show you."

Her hand stays in mine as we walk into the hall, and I open a door to a narrow stairway. "The attic?"

Technically, it's an attic, but it's been completely renovated. The floors are smooth and shiny, and a ceiling to floor mirror runs the length of the room. I paid the renovators double time to get this room done quickly, and the look on her face is worth every penny.

"The room will be filled with natural light during the day," I tell her, pointing out the skylight above us. "Now, anytime you feel like dancing, you have your own place."

Her eyes well. "I can't believe you did this."

"What, no argument this time?" I tease, pulling her into my arms. She shakes her head, speechless. "I love you, Ayda. I know living with me won't always be easy. There will be times when things are happening with ISH that I may not be able to tell you, but I swear I'll always keep you safe. I want you to be happy."

Tears pour down her cheeks when she peeks up at me. "I am happy."

I wipe her cheek. "I can tell. By the way, I turned the basement into a man cave."

"Okay." Her arms slide around my waist.

"You can't get in without the password."

Chuckling, she shakes her head. "What's the password?"

I lift the silver pendant from between her breasts, where it always lies, and her dark eyes stare into mine as she says, "Hummingbird?"

"Now I have to let you in." Something crashes downstairs, and raised voices filter up to us. "We'd better get down there. I promised them beer if they helped us move."

Laughing, we make our way back downstairs. A king sized mattress lies in the middle of the dining room floor, and Justus dives on it, smiling up at us as Sadie walks in.

"Knock knock!" she calls, and Ayda rushes over to her.

"Did you know about this?"

"Like I'd let him choose your furniture," Sadie scoffs.

"Hey, Sadist." Justus pats the mattress. "Help me test out their new bed." He turns to me. "You might want to go. I don't want to make you look bad." He regards Ayda. "You can stay."

"Do you want to kick his ass, or should I?" Sadie asks, and Ayda laughs.

"Why is he calling you Sadist?"

"Because he found out what happens when he waves his unicorn horn at the wrong girl."

It's almost dawn when Ayda and I finally crawl into our new bed. The house is a disaster of boxes and scattered items, but we'll worry about that tomorrow. Her warm little body presses against mine, and a contented sigh raises her chest, echoing my feelings exactly.

"Good night, Ayda."
"Good night, Dare."

The End

Don't miss Justus's story in book three of The In Safe Hands Series.
You can get it Here: http://mybook.to/Justus

ACKNOWLEDGMENTS

I hate writing acknowledgements because I know I'm going to leave someone out. So many people help me make my books the best they can be, from readers to bloggers and promoters. So please know if I don't mention you I really appreciate everything you do to help me and other Indie authors.

That being said, I'd like to thank Lissa Jay, Mayra Pena, and Susan Rollinson for beta reading, sometimes at the last minute, and saving me from embarrassing plot holes and ridiculous mistakes. I want to say thank you to few readers who always take the time to review, share and promote my books. Teresa Hall, Chantal Baxendale, and Michele loves books Jones, I'm pointing at you.

Thank you, Kim Ginsberg, for using those eagle eyes to beta and proofread my books.

The beautiful cover was made by Ally Hastings. Thank you so much, Ally.

Thanks to the members of the S.M. Shade Book Group for loving my books as much as I do (sometimes much more than I do) and sharing them constantly. Love you girls.

Last, but not least, thanks to all the book bloggers and page owners who make it possible for Indie authors to get their stories out there. We couldn't do it without you.

There's no way I can list the numerous blogs and pages that have reviewed and shared my books, but I want to call attention to a few who have been especially generous. Just One More Page, Saints and Sinners Books, Chicks Controlled by Books, and Romance Readers Retreat. You all rock so hard.

WHERE TO FIND S.M. SHADE

I love to connect with readers! Please find me at the following links:
Website www.authorsmshade.com
Amazon http://www.amazon.com/S.M.-Shade/e/B00HZZP9MM
Facebook page https://facebook.com/smshadebooks
Instagram https://www.instagram.com/authorsmshade/
Sign up for my newsletter http://bit.ly/1zNe5zu

I also have a private book group where no one outside of the group can see what you post or comment on. It's adults only and is a friendly place to discuss your favorite books and authors. Drama free. I also host an occasional giveaway, and group members get an early peek at covers, teasers, and exclusive excerpts.
You can join Shady Ladies here. https://www.facebook.com/groups/shadyladiesplace

MORE BY S.M. SHADE

THE TRAGIC DUET

Reading Order: Rock Star, Interrupted and Rock
Star, Unbroken
Rockstar. Enemies to Lovers. Single Dad. Alpha
Male.
Get Book One Here: http://mybook.to/RSI

Description:
I found my stillness, my space between breaths,
when I was a kid. The answer is simple. If it hurts,
I pour music on it.
After years of hard work, it's finally happening.
Tragic has a number one album and we've gone
from being discussed as one hit wonders to
hearing words like meteoric mentioned alongside
our name.

With two tours planned and another album on its way, we have a lot to look forward to. Playing in a different city every night, the shimmer and roar of the crowd, after parties and endless women.

My lifelong dream is in the palm of my hand until one phone call leaves everything hanging in the balance.

ROCK STAR, CONFINED

Standalone novel (spinoff of Tragic Duet)
Rockstar. Forced Proximity. Sweet Hero.
Get it Here: http://mybook.to/RSC

Description:
He's a musician on his way to the top. She's a woman scraping herself from rock bottom. An unbelievable year brings a love that changes everything.

Opening for Tragic, one of the most famous bands in the world, catapulted me from mediocre anonymity into the limelight. The leap from struggling musician to successful rock star happened quickly.

Just as suddenly as my career began, it slammed to a halt, stopped by a word uttered worldwide. Pandemic.

With my tour postponed, it looked like my year wasn't going to be a promising one, until I ended up quarantined with Geneva Rowe. Sexy, funny,

and a frustrating mystery, Geneva made the days fly by.
Now if only I could convince this stubborn woman we could have more than a temporary isolation fling.

THE DARK OF YOU

Standalone Dark Romance Novel (Stalker, Alpha Male)
Get it Here: http://mybook.to/TDOY

Description:
He stalked me.
He broke my peace, and I embraced the noise.
He tore apart all I believed about myself, and I reveled in the chaos.
He brought me back to life.
His promise remains with me, even now.
Wherever you are, I am.

THE VIOLENT CIRCLE SERIES (ROMANTIC COMEDY)

Reading Order: Scarlet Toys, Frat Hell, Clean Start, Zero F*cks, Level Up (Can be read as standalones)
Get Book One Here: http://mybook.to/Toysbook

Living on Violet Circle, a place that's less of a neighborhood and more of an insane asylum poured into the street, I thought I was prepared for anything. After you've seen a woman strip down at the laundry room to wash the clothes she's wearing, then saunter across the street naked, you've seen it all, right?

How naïve I was.

After the factory closed, leaving me and a good portion of the town unemployed, I took a job managing Scarlet Toys. I knew it wouldn't be a typical work environment, selling adult toys in a town more uptight than a constipated nun, but some things you just never see coming.

Like the protesters covered in poison ivy, screaming about smut peddlers.

Or a dancing dinosaur named Fappy.

Or the allure of the man standing in the center of all the chaos.

Wyatt Lawson, a six foot, four inch heap of muscle with a quick smile, ignited my interest in more than the available manager position. Like the missionary one. Or the rodeo. Maybe the side rider. What can I say? I'm an overachiever.

Let's just hope he doesn't scare easily.

THE SLUMMING IT SERIES (ROMANTIC COMEDY)

Spinoff series from Violent Circle.
Reading Order: Unsupervised, Overachiever, Incorrigible (Can be read as standalones)

Get Book One Here: http://mybook.to/
Unsupervised1

Description:
I'm in over my head. My decision to run from my
comfortable upper-class life was an impulsive
one, but I'm determined not to regret it. It's true I
have no car, have already been fired from my first
job, and can't cook without starting a fire, but I
can do this. Anything is better than the life I was
raised to lead as some successful man's arm
candy. I'm adjusting to my new circumstances
living with three roommates on Violent Circle, a
neighborhood known for being eccentric at best
and an insanity filled edible trip any other day.
On my own for the first time, I am quickly real-
izing there's a lot I need to learn, so signing up for
the adulting club that teaches life skills at college
seems like the perfect solution. That is, until I
walk into the first meeting and come face to face
with my gorgeous economics professor. Screw
learning how to change a tire or file your taxes.
There are much more adult things I want this man
to teach me.

ALL THAT REMAINS TRILOGY – AN MMF MENAGE SERIES

Reading Order: The Last Woman, Falling
Together, Infinite Ties

Get Book One Here: http://mybook.to/
TheLastWoman

Description:
When Abby Bailey meets former model and actor, Airen Holder, in a darkened department store, romance is the last thing on her mind. A plague has decimated the population, leaving Abby to raise her son alone in a world without electricity, clean water, or medical care. Her only priority is survival.

Traumatized by the horror of the past months, Abby and Airen become a source of comfort for one another. Damaged by her past and convinced Airen is out of her league, Abby is determined to keep their relationship platonic. However, Airen is a hard man to resist, especially after he risks his life to save hers.

When a man named Joseph falls unconscious in their yard, and Abby nurses him back to health, everything changes. How does love differ in this new post-apocalyptic world? Can three unlikely survivors live long enough to find their place in it?

Made in United States
Cleveland, OH
14 January 2025

13370993R00146